The Irregular at Magic High School

2

Tsutomu Sato

Illustration **Kana Ishida**

Illustration assistants **Jimmy Stone, Yasuko Suenaga**

Design **BEE-PEE**

Shizuku Kitayama

Miyuki's classmate in Class 1-A. Specializes in high-power vibration and acceleration magic. Cool and collected at a glance, her personality is the opposite of Honoka's.

Honoka Mitsui

Miyuki's classmate in Class 1-A. Specializes in controlling light using light wave–manipulation magic. Tends to cling rather strongly to her preconceived notions.

Miyuki Shiba

The younger sister of the Shiba siblings. Part of Class 1-A. An elite who entered Magic High as the top student. A Course 1 student, called a "Bloom," whose specialty is cooling magic. Her lovable only flaw is a severe brother complex.

"You care way more about food than your looks, don't you?"

Leonhard Saijou

Nicknamed "Leo." Part of Class 1-E, like Tatsuya. His father is half-Japanese and his mother a quarter. Specializes in hardening magic.

"Hey, let's go to the cake place after school today!"

"Okay, but... didn't we go with you yesterday?"

Erika Chiba

Tatsuya's classmate. Has a bright personality; a troublemaker who gets everyone involved. She comes from an old family famous for *kenjutsu*—a technique combining swords and magic.

Mizuki Shibata

Tatsuya's classmate. Sits next to the main character in class. Plain, but very popular among some upperclassmen as the "healing little-sister character." Because of her pushion-radiation sensitivity, she wears glasses, which is unusual in this day and age.

"Me, on the disciplinary committee? What's going on all of a sudden?"

Tatsuya Shiba

The older brother of the Shiba siblings. A new student of the National Magic University Affiliated First High School. Part of Class 1-E. One of the Course 2 students, mockingly called "Weeds." Specializes in designing Casting Assistant Devices (CADs).

"As the student council president, I am not satisfied with the current state of affairs.

"Both Course 1 and Course 2 students belong to this school, and these are the only three years any of us will have as students here."

Mayumi Saegusa

The student council president of First High. The eldest daughter of the Saegusas, one of the Ten Master Clans. Petite but glamorous. Referred to as a one-in-ten-years genius in the field of long-distance precision magic. Has a devilish personality.

"I am not as benevolent as my brother.

"Now, pray—

"...that you will at least keep your lives."

Casting Assistant Devices

Called CADs for short. Also referred to as *devices*, *assistants*, or *brooms*—that last term being both a witch's favorite magical tool and a play on the Japanese word for "magic operator." Broadly separated into two types, multipurpose and specialized, CADs are modern magicians' essential tools that store activation programs, which trigger magic in place of more traditional methods and tools such as spells, incantations, mudra, magic circles, spell books, and the like. The hardware in a CAD determines the expansion speed of its activation programs and the amount of information able to be expanded, while the embedded software determines how precise and effective the activation programs are. One can increase execution speed by simplifying the activation program and putting a bigger load on one's magic calculation region, but this ability is limited mostly to advanced magicians. For normal magicians, the CAD's processing speed is the most important factor in how fast they can execute magic.

Multipurpose CADs emphasize versatility. Up to ninety-nine types of activation programs may be installed on one CAD, regardless of what family each program belongs to. Bracelet-shaped CADs are the most popular, but many magicians also have ones shaped like smartphones, which are favored by advanced magicians working in the field who don't like having both hands tied when using them.

Specialized CADs sacrifice versatility to emphasize magic execution speed. Most are equipped with a targeting assistance subsystem. Up to nine activation programs can be installed at once, and they all have to be of the same family. Handguns and pistols are common shapes. Their muzzles are fitted with targeting assistance systems. The longer the muzzle on the CAD, the more effective the system is. The CAD Tatsuya owns, a customized Silver Horn model called "Trident," is one of these.

The
Irregular at
MagicHigh
School

The Irregular at Magic High School

ENROLLMENT
Part II

2

Tsutomu Sato

Illustration Kana Ishida

YEN ON

NEW YORK

THE IRREGULAR AT MAGIC HIGH SCHOOL
TSUTOMU SATO

Translation by Andrew Prowse
Cover art by Kana Ishida

This book is a work of fiction. Names, characters, places, and incidents are the product of the author's imagination or are used fictitiously. Any resemblance to actual events, locales, or persons, living or dead, is coincidental.

MAHOUKA KOUKOU NO RETTOUSEI Vol. 2
© TSUTOMU SATO 2011
Edited by ASCII MEDIA WORKS
First published in Japan in 2011 by KADOKAWA CORPORATION, Tokyo.
English translation rights arranged with KADOKAWA CORPORATION, Tokyo,
through Tuttle-Mori Agency, Inc., Tokyo.

English translation © 2016 by Yen Press, LLC

Yen On
1290 Avenue of the Americas
New York, NY 10104

Visit us at yenpress.com
facebook.com/yenpress
twitter.com/yenpress
yenpress.tumblr.com

First Yen On Edition: August 2016

Yen On is an imprint of Yen Press, LLC.
The Yen On name and logo are trademarks of Yen Press, LLC.

The publisher is not responsible for websites (or their content) that are not owned by the publisher.

Library of Congress Cataloging-in-Publication Data
Names: Satou, Tsutomu, author. | Ishida, Kana, illustrator. | Prowse, Andrew (Andrew R.), translator.
Title: The irregular at Magic High School. Volume 2, Enrollment. Part II / Tsutomu Satou.
Other titles: Mahōka kōkō no rettosei. English | Enrollment. Part II
Description: First Yen On edition. | New York, NY : Yen On, 2016–
Identifiers: LCCN 2016019949 | ISBN 9780316390293 (paperback)
Subjects: | CYAC: Brothers and sisters—Fiction. | Magic—Fiction. | High schools—Fiction. |
    Schools—Fiction. | Japan—Fiction. | Science fiction.
Classification: LCC PZ7.1.S265 Is 2016 | DDC [Fic]—dc23 LC record available at
    https://lccn.loc.gov/2016019949

ISBN: 978-0-316-39029-3

10 9 8 7 6 5

LSC-C

Printed in the United States of America

The Irregular at MagicHigh School

ENROLLMENT
PART II

An irregular older brother with a certain flaw.
An honor roll younger sister who is perfectly flawless.

When the two siblings enrolled in Magic High School,
a dramatic life unfolded—

Glossary

Magic High School

A nickname for the high schools affiliated with the National Magic University. There are nine schools throughout the nation. Of them, First High through Third High each adopt a system of Course 1 and Course 2 students to split up its two hundred incoming freshmen.

Blooms, Weeds

Slang terms used at First High to display the gap between Course 1 and Course 2 students. Course 1 student uniforms feature an eight-petaled emblem embroidered on the left breast, but Course 2 student uniforms do not.

CAD (Casting Assistant Device)

A device that simplifies magic casting. Magical programming is recorded within. There are many types and forms, some specialized and others multipurpose.

Course 1 student emblem

Miyuki Shiba's CAD

Tatsuya Shiba's CAD

Four Leaves Technology (FLT)

A domestic CAD manufacturer. Originally more famous for magic engineering products than for finished products, the development of the Silver model has made them much more widely known as a maker of CADs.

Taurus Silver

A genius engineer said to have advanced specialized CAD software by a decade in just a single year.

Eidos (individual information bodies)

Originally a term from Greek philosophy. In modern magic, *eidos* refers to the information bodies accompanying events. They are a record of those events existing in the world, and they can be called the footprints that events record upon the world. The definition of *magic* as it applies to its modern form is that of a technology that alters these events themselves by altering the eidos composing them.

Idea (information body dimension)

Originally a term from Greek philosophy; pronounced "ee-dee-ah." In modern magic, *Idea* refers to the platform upon which eidos are recorded. Magic is primarily a technology that outputs a magic program onto the Idea and rewrites the eidos composing them.

Activation program

The blueprints of magic and the programming that constructs it. Activation programs are stored in a compressed format in CADs. The magician sends a psionic wave into the CAD, which then expands the data and uses it to convert the activation program into a signal, then returns it to the magician.

Psions (thought particles)

Massless particles belonging to the dimension of spirit phenomena. The information particles that record awareness and thought results. Eidos are considered the theoretical basis for modern magic, while activation programs and magic programs are the technology forming its practical basis—these are all bodies of information that are made up of psions.

Pushions (spirit particles)

Massless particles belonging to the dimension of spirit phenomena. Their existence has been confirmed, but their true form and function have yet to be elucidated. In general, magicians are only able to "sense" energized pushions.

Character

Tatsuya Shiba

Class 1-E. A Course 2
(irregular) student, who are
mockingly called Weeds.

Miyuki Shiba

Class 1-A.
Tatsuya's younger sister;
enrolled as the top student.

Leonhard Saijou

Class 1-E.
Tatsuya's classmate.

Erika Chiba

Class 1-E.
Tatsuya's classmate.

Mizuki Shibata

Class 1-E.
Tatsuya's classmate.

[6]

The club committee headquarters, just before closing time.

"—And that concludes my report on the incident in which the *kenjutsu* club interrupted the kendo club's recruitment demonstration."

Tatsuya had just finished relating the full story of the incident he had witnessed and experienced: the argument between Sayaka Mibu and Takeaki Kirihara, their personal struggle, and the sequence of events culminating in an attempted brawl where Tatsuya had taken on the *kenjutsu* club by himself. Three students were in front of him.

"I just can't believe you fought over ten people and came away unscathed..."

Facing him on the right was the student council president, Mayumi Saegusa.

"Fourteen, to be exact. I guess I should expect nothing less from one of Kokonoe's disciples."

In the middle was the disciplinary committee chairwoman—and in a sense, Tatsuya's boss—Mari Watanabe. Her comment was accompanied by a jovial laugh. It was amused rather than derisive, and not sarcastic in any way. She wasn't entirely honest with how she expressed her emotions, but her praise sounded sincere.

Mayumi and Mari were impressed (?) with how, after he'd subdued Kirihara, he'd dealt with the frenzied group of *kenjutsu* club members without actually attacking them at all, purely by defending himself. Tatsuya, however, didn't truly feel he had shown any praiseworthy skills.

He was out of touch with the expected skill level of average high school students. What he'd done wouldn't have even been up to the Yakumo temple's gatekeepers' standards. He didn't get it—what was so good about dispatching fourteen people at once and being unharmed?

Instead, he was paying more attention to the male senior on the left facing him. That was probably Katsuto Juumonji, head of the club committee—the eldest child of an elite Numbers family, with the *juu* in his name written with the character for "ten."

He's like a giant boulder...

He stood around six feet one, so Tatsuya didn't need to bend his neck to look at his face. But he had a bulky chest, wide shoulders, and muscles that bulged distinctly through his uniform. And his striking physical characteristics weren't the only thing on his side. The very *density* of his existence had to be measured on an entirely different scale. It was like he contained every factor humans possessed, compressed into the smallest space possible.

He was one of the three giants of First High, along with Mayumi and Mari, and his appearance and impression were more than enough to convince Tatsuya of that.

"You didn't see how it started, right?" asked Mari, having calmed herself.

Snapping back to reality, he summoned up his memories of the incident he'd just finished reporting on yet again. "Yes," he confirmed. "However, I don't know who started it. The kendo club says Kirihara provoked it, and the *kenjutsu* club claims the kendo club made the first move."

Tatsuya had only come in during the start of Sayaka and Kirihara's argument. He and Erika had left their spots on the viewing deck and were just about to leave the gymnasium when they heard noises that sounded like people fighting over something. From that far away, though, he couldn't hear what they were saying. By the time he'd cut through the crowd there and seen for himself, it was already a touchy situation, with Sayaka and Kirihara staring each other down.

"Perhaps that's why you didn't intervene right at the start?" That was Mayumi. Katsuto had been just listening the entire time.

"I did intend to disrupt them if I decided things were dangerous," assured Tatsuya, though conditionally. "My thoughts were that they could deal with it themselves if all that resulted were a few scrapes and bruises."

The reason Tatsuya had taken an observer's viewpoint at the beginning, like Mayumi noted, was because he didn't know which of them needed to be stopped. There was always the option of stopping both, but one of two conditions would need to be fulfilled for him to do so: Either there still needed to be enough room to talk them down, or there needed to be a justification for overpowering them despite how famous—or notorious—they were. Neither of those had applied in this case.

That wasn't his only reason, however. A disciplinary committee member's job, at least as far as Tatsuya understood, was to take control of situations involving acts of magic-based violence. Though the contest between Sayaka and Kirihara was a personal one, it started as a battle of sword skills. There had been no magic involved. If Kirihara hadn't used any—like his High-Frequency Blade—then Tatsuya probably would have stuck to his guns and watched it play out.

"...Well, that's fine. We obviously can't be there every time someone gets into a fight. We don't have enough people for that," said Mari. Her remark was rooted in the rule that the club committee—not the disciplinary committee—was the one that dealt with recruitment-related trouble. Neither Mayumi nor Katsuto had any objection to that. "What did you do with Kirihara after subduing him?"

"His collarbone was broken, so I gave him to the health-care committee. It was a light enough wound that magic could heal it quickly, though. He admitted his fault in the nurse's office, so I decided no further action was necessary."

In reality, getting hit with a *shinai* wouldn't do any more than put cracks in a bone—his collarbone had been broken when Tatsuya slammed him into the floor. That, however, didn't need to be said, so he didn't.

Mari hadn't been present when Kirihara was hurt, nor did she see his wounds firsthand. She wouldn't have known better. "Hmm... All right. We're leaving the choice to take legal action to the other party anyway." Tatsuya nodded briefly, and Mari looked at Katsuto. "That's that, Juumonji. The disciplinary committee won't be bringing this incident to the punishment committee."

"I appreciate your generosity. The High-Frequency Blade is a highly lethal spell, and he used it in the open for a petty reason. Normally he'd face expulsion for this, but I think he knows that. I will give him a good talking-to and make sure he learns his lesson."

"Thanks," said Mari. Katsuto bowed lightly, and she nodded back.

"Will the kendo club be satisfied with that?" asked Mayumi, worried.

"They're equally guilty. They took the bait and got into the fight," answered Mari, cutting down her concern with a single stroke. "They have no right to complain."

The disciplinary committee chairwoman had delivered her judgment, the club committee leader had accepted it, and the student council president had no objections. That marked the end of the incident.

Tatsuya listened to their exchange with a detached attitude. It wasn't his job to smother any smoldering flames of discontent. He conveyed his position by asking for permission to withdraw. "Chairwoman, may I leave?"

"Oh, wait, one more thing I want to know first." Mari's tone of voice was casual; she didn't seem to want Tatsuya to do anything else. For today, anyway. "Was Kirihara the only one who used magic?"

"That's right," nodded Tatsuya simply.

More precisely, Kirihara was the only one who had *successfully executed* magic—but Tatsuya wasn't possessed of the hardworking spirit he would have needed to explain the particulars.

"I see. Good job, then. You can leave."

With permission to go, Tatsuya put the club committee headquarters behind him.

After leaving the club committee HQ, Tatsuya planned to head straight for the student council room.

There was only a little sunlight left. Regardless of how talented with magic they might have been, it was inappropriate for girls of Miyuki's age to walk around on their own at this hour. Miyuki would never have ventured to leave Tatsuya at school and go home anyway.

Halfway there, however, he was forced to revise those plans.

The club committee was in a separate building from the main school building, where the student council room was. To get to the former from the latter, you needed to go out to the courtyard (no need to change into your shoes—the custom of wearing slippers had all but disappeared) then go around the entrance. But as he turned the corner he found familiar faces there to greet him.

"Oh, hey there! Good work!"

"Tatsuya!"

The first one to say something was Erika, but the first one to run over to him was Miyuki. The others looked surprised at her unexpected agility.

"How was work? I heard you did a lot today."

"It was nothing much. Miyuki, you probably had a harder time."

Separated from Miyuki only by the bag he was holding in front of his waist, she looked up into his eyes; he stroked her hair a few times as her look asked him to. She narrowed her eyes comfortably, but didn't turn them away from her brother.

"You know, I get that you're brother and sister, but…" muttered Leo, walking over to the two of them and glancing subtly away with an embarrassed look.

"You two look kind of picturesque…" Next to him, Mizuki blushed, but looked at them with a penetrating gaze.

Erika narrowed her eyes at Leo and Mizuki. "Hey… Just what are you two expecting from them, anyway?" She lifted her hands to the left and right in an exaggerated shrug, looked down, and slowly shook her head from side to side. That kind of action was obviously feigned, but it looked good when Erika did it. "Didn't you *just* say they're brother and sister?"

The implication in her repeating what Leo said as Erika stared at him seemed to be understood by both Leo and Mizuki. Their flustered reaction spoke to that.

"D-d-d-d-don't be stupid! I-I'm not expecting anything!"

"Th-th-th-th-th-th-that's right, Erika! D-don't say strange things!"

"…Okay, okay. I'll be nice this time and drop the subject."

Nevertheless, if Erika hadn't made her wisecrack, Leo's and Mizuki's misbegotten notions probably would have run away with them.

Ignorant of Erika's solitary struggle, Tatsuya finally removed his hand from his sister's hair and looked at the three of them. Miyuki followed suit with a reluctant expression.

—The fact that she made that kind of expression all the time was exactly why they were getting those strange ideas.

But Tatsuya, without any expression or action that could have been linked to such flights of fancy, addressed his friends apologetically with an honest look and said, "Sorry—did I keep you waiting?"

With the odd atmosphere swept away, Leo suddenly broke into a smile and shook his head. "Don't be so formal, Tatsuya. This isn't the time for apologies."

"My club orientation just ended a few minutes ago. I wasn't waiting at all!" Mizuki, too, gave an affable smile and rejected Tatsuya's apology as unnecessary.

"He just got out of club, too. Don't worry about it," Erika replied arrogantly with her usual mischievous smirk.

Leo, Mizuki, and Erika all welcomed him with a smile.

Tatsuya quickly realized the truth was the opposite of what they said, but they were only doing it out of consideration. He wouldn't bring their efforts to naught. "It's late, so why don't we grab a snack somewhere? I'll treat you, as long as it's less than a thousand yen."

The denominations of monetary units had been changed twice now, so the value of currency had been about the same for a century. One thousand yen for a high school student was a bit on the high side, but still an appropriate line to draw.

It was an invitation offered in lieu of any further apologies. All present understood as much, and refrained from acting needlessly reserved.

In a café different from the one they'd used on the day of the entrance ceremony, the five students enthusiastically spoke of the various experiences they'd had today—like the clubs they'd entered, having to mind their club rooms in the absence of others and being bored, and people hitting on them under the guise of recruitment. But of the most interest was the grand tale of Tatsuya's arrest.

"—This Kirihara sophomore—he used magic with rank B lethality, didn't he? And you didn't get hurt by it?"

"It may be deadly, but the High-Frequency Blade has a fairly narrow effective range," answered Tatsuya to the blindly impressed Leo, shrinking back a bit. "If you leave aside the fact that you can't touch *any* part of the blade, it's no different from a well-sharpened katana. It's fairly easy to deal with spells like that."

"But that means you stopped someone with a sword using only your bare hands! Isn't that really dangerous?"

"It's all right, Mizuki. You don't need to worry about my brother."

"You seem pretty relaxed, Miyuki," remarked Erika. Miyuki's expression did indeed have an unnatural ease to it as she soothed Mizuki, whose own face had clouded over.

"Yeah, considering you handled over ten guys, your skills can only be called excellent—but Kirihara's were certainly nothing to shake a stick at. In fact, he was a cut above everybody else there. Miyuki, you really weren't worried?"

"No," answered Miyuki instantly and without hesitation. "There can't possibly be anyone who can best my brother."

"—Umm…" Even Erika didn't know what to say to that. She had seen Tatsuya's skills firsthand when it happened. Even from her point of view, Kirihara's swordsmanship had been merciless and keen. Tatsuya would have known that his blade's sharpness rivaled that of an actual sword. And still, he didn't use any more energy than he absolutely needed to, which had betrayed the complete absence of any nervousness or fear in his mind. He had closed in on Kirihara faster than Kirihara could bring down his *shinai*, grabbed its hilt, twisted its wielder's wrist, and thrown him to the floor like it was an aikido technique. In fact, Erika mused that it might have *been* an actual technique—one meant to disarm an opponent.

Calling his skills master class wasn't an exaggeration. Tatsuya had already learned enough that he'd earned the title of master. Or, at the very least, something close to it. Still, though, Erika would have been lying a little if she said she wasn't worried.

"…I'm not doubting your ability, Tatsuya," began Mizuki, "but the High-Frequency Blade isn't just a normal sword. Doesn't it create ultrasonic waves?"

"Oh yeah, I've heard of it, too," remarked Leo. "Don't some people use earplugs when they cast it so they don't get sick on the waves? Well, I guess you would have already considered that."

"That's not it. It isn't just because of my brother's superb physical abilities," answered Miyuki to their worried questions. She, however, seemed to be holding back a smile. "Nullifying magic programs is my brother's forte."

Erika lost no time in getting a word in. "Nullifying magic programs? Not, like, Information Boost or Area Interference?"

"That's right," nodded Miyuki meaningfully. Tatsuya gave a resigned smile.

Erika looked at them in turn and muttered, half in admiration and half in astonishment, "That, uh, sounds like a pretty rare skill to have."

"Yes. At least, I don't think they teach it in high school. Not everyone who learns it can actually use it. Erika, right after my brother ran out there, did you feel like the floor was wobbling?"

"Hmm... It didn't do much to me, but I think there were kids who came down with a bad case of motion sickness. Come to think of it, it wasn't just at the start. Smaller ones kept happening during the fight, too, I think..."

"That was my brother's doing. Tatsuya, you used Cast Jamming, didn't you?"

"You always see right through me, Miyuki."

"Well, of course. I know everything about you."

"Wait, wait, wait!" interrupted Leo, grimacing as the two exchanged smiles—one dry, and one happy. "That's not how siblings talk to each other. You're even past the level of a married couple!"

"You think so?" "Is that so?" answered Tatsuya and Miyuki in perfect harmony. For a full second, Leo froze, then collapsed onto the table entirely drained of energy.

"...It would be absurd to try and get a word in when they're in newlywed mode like that," said Erika quietly to him. "I told you, you never stood a chance."

"Yeah, I was wrong..." Leo answered, also quietly, sitting back up.

"This is not something I would willingly have people say about us..."

"Oh, but it's true," said Miyuki soothingly and fluidly. "My brother and I are bound together by strong fraternal love."

This time, both Erika and Leo fell onto the table at the same time. "Ghah!" Leo even made his own sound effect as though blood were spurting from his nose, expressing his sentiments.

And still Miyuki didn't stop. "I do adore my brother more than anyone else in the world." She moved her chair and brought her body near Tatsuya's, then passionately looked up into his eyes, all as if putting on a show for their friends.

"Ah, okay, I think I'm going home now," said Erika, utterly sulking, her cheek still plastered to the table.

"Miyuki, don't get carried away, all right? There's, let's see... approximately one person who doesn't understand it's a joke."

"..." "..." "..."

After Tatsuya grinned drily and chided Miyuki, she, Erika, and Leo all looked toward the last person present.

"...Huh? What? A joke?" Mizuki's gaze was downcast, and her face flushed red—her eyes were even darting from left to right. Someone sighed.

"...Well, that's what makes Mizuki who she is, I guess."

At Erika's heartwarming murmur, Mizuki groaned, her face turning red for a different reason.

Then, despite having been strung along himself, Leo couldn't seem to take the creepy atmosphere any longer, and forcibly brought the conversation back to its original topic. "...By the way, you mentioned Cast Jamming, didn't you?"

"Well, it's a secret, but yes." This wasn't a topic Tatsuya much wanted to discuss, but he probably cared more about dispelling the air that had formed around them. He went along with Leo's suggestion without any other choice.

"Cast Jamming... That's jamming magic waves, right?"

"They're not waves," retorted Leo, though it was better left unsaid.

II

"It's a figure of speech!" Erika shot with a straight face, turning her gaze back to Tatsuya.

Cast Jamming was a type of magic that prevented magic programs from going to work on the information bodies called eidos that were incidental to phenomena. It could be broadly classified as having the same properties as typeless magic.

There was another spell called Area Interference that also nullified an opponent's magic. This spell used a magic program that specified only interference strength in a fixed area around the caster and prevented all alterations to information in that area. Using it would shut down the other person's magic program interference. Cast Jamming, however, worked by scattering large amounts of psionic waves, or psi-waves—a technique to prevent the process by which magic programs interacted with eidos.

In a way, Area Interference "reserved" magic in an area and prevented other casters from interrupting with *their* magic. Fundamentally, you needed more magical influence than the opponent.

On the other hand, Cast Jamming affected the metaphorical radio tower that other users tried to upload data to. By requesting a huge amount of access, it would reduce their upload speed to almost nothing. One's magical influence wasn't that much of a problem. In exchange, the psionic noise could obstruct all four families and eight types of magic—following with the radio base example, by rapidly and irregularly changing the frequency of the waves. It would require one to create enough waves to completely block off an entire region with just one transmission antenna.

"But don't you need a special rock for that? Anti…anti-something."

Erika broke off at an odd point, unable to remember the proper noun. Mizuki, who had managed to revive herself, threw her a lifeboat. "It's antinite, Erika. Tatsuya, do you own any antinite? I thought it was really expensive."

Antinite was known to be a substance that could generate enough psionic noise to fulfill this condition. While it was theorized that a magician could create the noise needed for Cast Jamming with their own calculations, it was nevertheless difficult to implement.

Unlike Area Interference, Cast Jamming would obstruct the caster's own magic as well. Even if a magician tried to construct the noise for Cast Jamming consciously, his or her unconscious would instinctively reject it. (The magic calculation region formed within a person's unconscious, so it prioritized unconscious control over conscious control.)

Because of this, antinite—which could generate the required noise just by emitting psions—was thought to be indispensable for using Cast Jamming.

Tatsuya's answer, however, overruled common sense. "No, I don't have any. It's a military-grade product in the first place, after all. The problem isn't the price—civilians can't get it."

"Huh? But you just said you used Cast Jamming..." Erika was the one who actually spoke, but both she and Leo looked at him incredulously.

He paused for a moment, his face troubled. Then he leaned over the table and said lowly, "Uh, this is all off the record, okay?" The other three, now drawn in, leaned forward as well, nodding in seriousness. "It's not *technically* Cast Jamming. What I used is Specified Magic Jamming. It operates under the same theory."

Upon hearing Tatsuya's whispers, Mizuki looked startled and blinked a few times over. "Umm... I didn't know magic like that existed."

Erika was the one to directly answer that question. "I don't think it does," she said. "Doesn't that mean you worked out the theory for a new spell?" Once again, her voice sounded more appalled than impressed or shocked.

There were plenty of magicians who used their own, original magic—and plenty of up-and-coming ones who specialized in original magic from a young age. However, that was a case of them

instinctively—or intuitively—coming up with magic in a natural way. There weren't many magicians who could construct new magic from a theoretical standpoint.

Magic depended heavily on the use of one's unconscious.

While it may have been easy to retroactively attach a theory to magic one could use unconsciously, creating a new spell on a theoretical level—even if it was a simple variation on an existing one—demanded a complete and total understanding of the spell's construction and the principles it operated under.

Someone the age of a high school student formulating a theory for a new spell wasn't just abnormal—it made no sense.

"It was less me working it out and more a chance discovery," answered Tatsuya, smiling at Erika's straightforward reaction. "You know that in most cases, when you try to use two CADs at once, the psi-waves interfere with each other and the magic doesn't go off, right?"

"Yeah, I learned that the hard way," nodded Leo.

"Whoa, that's way out of your league," muttered Erika, appalled at Leo's words.

"What was that?!"

"You were trying to use two *brooms* to cast magic in parallel! If you thought you could pull off a high-level technique like that, then you *were* way out of your league."

"Oh, shut up. I thought I could! Since I can activate multiple spells as long as they're my type, you know."

"No way. Seriously. Amazing."

"…You've made your point already, so quit talking in monotone. It's making me even angrier."

"H-hey, come on, let's listen to what Tatsuya has to say!"

"…"

"…Hmph."

Erika and Leo looked away from each other.

Tatsuya shrugged at Mizuki, whose gaze was wandering to and

fro. "I'm fine with stopping here…but you want me to keep going? I don't mind, I guess…

"The psionic interference waves emitted when using two CADs at the same time, just like with Cast Jamming, get sent to the Idea, which contains the eidos of events near the magician. With one CAD you expand an activation program for the spell that will do the obstructing, then with the other CAD you expand an activation program in the opposite direction. Then you make multiple copies of the activation programs without actually converting them into magic programs. If you release the resultant psionic signal waves as type-less magic, then—to a certain extent—you can block the activation of spells that are the same type as the two magic programs you *would* have created from the activation programs with each CAD.

"Even for persistent spells like High-Frequency Blade, you can't maintain the magic program's effects indefinitely. At some point, you'll have to expand another activation program and redo it. I just happened to figure out the exact timing to do that in this case."

"Seriously…" whispered Leo. His monotonous tone revealed that it wasn't only his expression that was dumbfounded.

All of a sudden, Mizuki coughed. She had nearly choked on her straw—she'd been slurping from it even after her glass had been emptied. Her emotions seemed to finally snap out of her trance because of the painful coughing, and her face gave way to shock.

Erika furrowed her brow, silently thinking about something. It didn't look like anything particularly pleasant given the grim look on her face, but it didn't seem like she was particularly unhappy with anything.

"…I have basically no idea what you would actually do, but I think I understand the logic behind it. But why is this all off the record? If you patented it you could probably make money off it," said Leo, managing to restart his thought processes and evidently not satisfied.

In response to his confusion, Tatsuya grinned bitterly—more bitterly than happily. "First, because this technique is incomplete. It just blocks the spell the enemy is in the middle of activating; it isn't like they can't use magic at *all*, it just gets harder. The user, however, *can't* use magic at all after using this. That in itself is a fatal flaw, but the more important issue is that it can obstruct casting without using antinite."

"...Why is that a problem?" asked Leo, more unsatisfied than suspicious.

Erika, who had been lost in thought, scolded him in a fairly serious manner. "You're an idiot. Of course it's a problem. Magic is currently something that national defense and peacekeeping forces need at all costs. If some easy, magic-nullifying technique that didn't need expensive antinite or a lot of magic power started to spread, it could shake the foundations of society."

"Those are my thoughts as well. There are even radical groups advocating for the abolition of magic on the grounds that it's somehow a source of discrimination. Not much antinite gets produced, so it doesn't realistically present a threat. Until they can find a way to deal with it, I don't want to go public with this Cast Jamming imitation."

Leo nodded a few times, his curiosity appearing sated at last. For some reason, Mizuki was nodding with the same expression. "That's amazing," she sighed in admiration. "You thought so far ahead."

"Yeah, I would've probably gone straight for the fame and popularity!" sighed Leo in turn.

Miyuki gave a soft, reserved smile at him. "I believe my brother is thinking a little too hard about it, to be honest. It isn't as though just *anyone* can read an activation program as an opponent is expanding it, or project CAD interference waves. But I suppose that is just how he is."

"...How I am? Are you calling me lazy and indecisive?"

"Well, I don't know. What do you think, Erika?" said Miyuki with feigned ignorance, throwing the ball to Erika.

"I don't know. I, for one, want to hear Mizuki's opinion on it," said Erika in an affected tone, tossing the ball back into Mizuki's court.

"Huh? Um, I, well…"

"No one's going to disagree for me…?" With Tatsuya's rueful stare turned on them, Miyuki constructed a cheerful smile and averted her eyes, Erika hid her face behind her menu, and Mizuki's eyes darted back and forth, unsure—but from none of them came any help.

Tatsuya was on the run again today.

The new club member recruitment week (which was the fancy term for all this horseplay) was already on its fourth day. Though perhaps the word *still* would have been more apt than *already*…but regardless, it was busy. It seemed backward to him that it was far more exhausting *after* school than during classes, but unfortunately, nobody would listen to his objections.

It made him wonder what resort in which time period these barkers belonged to—or rather, these solicitors—or sorry, the *recruitment officers*. Instead of cutting through the jam-packed schoolyard, he avoided it (he'd learned on the second day there was no point in volunteering himself for labor like that) and ran toward the location from which he'd received the report of trouble.

On the way there, from the other side of the tent-forested area in the shade of some trees, he detected signs that someone was about to fire magic at him.

It wouldn't interfere with him directly—it seemed to be a spell to upturn the ground at his feet (more accurately, to shift the ground under his feet on top of the ground to the front and back).

Not again, he thought, sick of it. He must have stood out too much on the first day. Now people were bullying him like this all the time.

Thanks (?) to that, though, he'd gotten used to it. In an unhurried, matter-of-fact way, he activated his Cast Jamming imitation and matched it with the spell's type. He actually possessed a way of nullifying the spell more easily, but the kind of aftereffects it would cause made it highly probable he'd have a pain dealing with it later. One of the valuable teachings he'd acquired during his short life thus far was that cutting corners never led to anything good.

His psionic wave spread and dispersed, and the magic program dissipated without going off.

Without stopping even a moment, he took a sudden turn.

Cutting corners really wasn't ever a good thing. Maybe it was because he'd let things be since they didn't actually harm him, but the number of times he'd experienced magic harassment like this had been escalating rapidly. He'd been ignoring it out of his responsibilities as a disciplinary officer, but at this point, he thought it was okay to start taking his self-defense more seriously.

His opponent, however, was shrewd as well. Right as Tatsuya turned toward him, he leaped out of the shade with speed impossible by pure physical talent. Whoever it was had probably prepared a high-speed running spell beforehand by combining movement magic and anti-inertial magic. The issue with such spells was that your legs wouldn't normally be able to keep up with the speed and you'd fall, but the culprit seemed to be quite physically fit.

Tatsuya judged it would be hard to apprehend the person in a short time and canceled his pursuit.

The only clues he'd gotten were the tall, thin stature of the culprit and the white wristband, lined with red on blue on either edge, he wore on his right hand.

A week passed.

The new club member recruitment week had been a torrent of events for Tatsuya.

He was probably the busiest out of all the members of the disciplinary committee.

—For slightly different reasons than you might think.

Takeaki Kirihara, whom Tatsuya had subdued on the first day, was apparently one of the school's most hopeful competitive magic athletes. Some held the opinion that Tatsuya could dispatch him so easily because Kirihara had been hurt during his duel with Sayaka Mibu before Tatsuya had gotten involved. However, most of the students who weren't aware of the finer details of the competitive magic athlete certainly weren't too pleased with the incident where the regular athlete had been beaten by a freshman—and a Weed, at that.

As a result...

"Tatsuya, you got disciplinary committee stuff again today?" asked Leo, picking up his bag and getting ready to go home.

"I'm off today. Looks like I'll finally get a break."

"You did a bang-up job, after all."

"I'm not at all happy about it, though," sighed Tatsuya glumly.

Leo was clearly holding back laughter. "You're a celebrity now, Tatsuya! The mysterious freshman who went undefeated against all the regular magic athletes in the room—that's what they're saying."

"Mysterious? Why...?"

"There's one theory that you're a hired killer sent by a magic opposition group!" That was Erika poking her face into the conversation, also just about ready to go home.

"Who on earth would spread such irresponsible rumors...?"

"Me!"

"Hey!"

"I'm joking, of course."

"Give me a break... You're really nasty, you know that?"

"But it's true that the rumors exist."

Tatsuya ended up sighing once again at the substance of the rumors Erika had brought to him. He didn't think anyone would readily believe such groundless stories—at least he didn't *want* to. It was fully within the realm of expectation that someone or other would take advantage of the talk and make a move on him, though.

"That was quite a sigh!"

"No empathy at all, I see… Try putting yourself in my shoes. I almost died three times this week!"

"No thank you!" Leo wasn't trying to hide the amusement from his face. Tatsuya felt an urge to punch him in the nose, but instead he just breathed a third sigh.

Takeaki Kirihara, viewed as the top of the sophomore class in terms of practical ability, was the next ace of the *kenjutsu* club. And a freshman Weed had beaten him. As stated before, the news surprised and infuriated those steeped in a superficial stance of them being some "chosen ones." They directed their completely unfair anger and resentment at Tatsuya. Currently, people bent on misdirected acts of retaliation were coming out of the woodwork.

Nevertheless, instigating any direct fights would mark them as targets to be purged. He was backed by the disciplinary committee chairwoman. Everyone, even those without intimate details of the situation, could easily imagine the student council and the club committee coming to his aid.

Then what should they do? The standard move would be to pretend like it was an accident. And that's what they did. They would wait for Tatsuya to approach on his patrol, then create an intentional quarrel. When he stepped in to mediate, he would be hit with magical attacks made to look like misfires. That seemed to be the pattern.

From Tatsuya's point of view, incidents were suddenly breaking out wherever he went, one after another. It was unbearable. But as long as he was a disciplinary committee member, he couldn't ignore them and pass by—he needed to make an effort to bring the situations under control.

On top of that, people were just flinging magic at him at random, too. He was able to nullify most of them before their effects manifested and escape danger, but there were some he couldn't completely quell, too.

He'd known on the first day that people seemed to be after him, but he couldn't do anything until he discovered proof that it was all secretly connected—and by the time he did, recruitment week would be over.

In other words, he couldn't help running right into every trap.

He had only discovered a culprit during that one incident on the fourth day, but he had fled as well. The person was, after all, a student studying at the elite First High. In general, everyone here was extremely skilled in their methods. Tatsuya got the feeling, though, that the time, place, and objective for their superb abilities couldn't have been more thoroughly mistaken.

"...When I think about it, it's amazing I didn't get hurt..."

"They're putting the restriction back on carrying devices around today, so you don't have any more to worry about, right?" said Mizuki, trying to console him.

"I sure hope so," said Tatsuya, taking the opportunity to nod.

The student council may have had off-seasons, but it had no days off. It didn't work on a shift system, after all. Miyuki had to work at the student council again today. And for the siblings, leaving one at school and going home alone wasn't an option. From an objective spectator's point of view, it was their own fault they were teased as having a brother/sister complex.

Nevertheless—"I'm sorry, Tatsuya. I will need to make you wait for me..."—as long as they still had the good sense to feel guilty over making the other wait, they could still be saved.

"Don't worry about it... Well, you probably can't do that, can you..." Tatsuya said, smiling, patting his sister's head a couple times.

It would be more apt to call it a *pet* than a *pat*. His hands were gentle, and Miyuki bashfully—but comfortably—narrowed her eyes. —While walking through a hallway with students going home.

Their display of intimacy was prone to being misunderstood (?). The glances cast toward the two heading for the student council room were a mix of goodwill and malice. However, there was a marked difference in them from the all-too-common stares given to couples that were too friendly with each other, and Tatsuya pulled his hand away when he felt the malicious ones.

When he walked with Miyuki like this...

Until last week, the greater portion of those mean looks would have been ridiculing. Now, there was a hateful antipathy...and, peeking out from behind it, fear. Not the awe given to the strong...but the fear given to the unknown. The Course 2 students who should have been *relieved* at his actions were doing the same.

All that said, this was the first time this week he was spoken to by someone he didn't know.

"Shiba?"

Tatsuya and Miyuki turned around in sync. His physical abilities were clearly superior. The reason they reacted at the same time regardless was because Miyuki's act was done out of reflex, whereas Tatsuya hadn't been completely sure the person had been talking to *him*.

"Hello. And pleased to meet you, I suppose?"

It was a fairly pretty girl with medium-length hair pulled back in a ponytail. A strange hairstyle, but Tatsuya remembered seeing her face. "You're right, nice to meet you. Your name is Mibu, right?"

She was the sophomore in the kendo club who was essentially the beginning of his week of violence—and one of the parties involved in the kendo club intrusion incident.

Tatsuya stopped, and she approached with unhesitating movements. Either she was fearless by nature, or free of worry because he was younger. Or maybe she held him in disdain for the same reason. Whichever the case was, it was certainly better than awkward reservation.

Miyuki aligned her movements with the upperclassman as she stopped before her brother and took a half-step back. She was in a spot just out of Tatsuya's focus, but naturally inside it if he turned the slightest bit away.

"I'm Sayaka Mibu. I'm in Class E, same as you." Tatsuya's eyes were naturally drawn to Sayaka's left breast. Sewn onto her green blazer was a plain green pocket. He realized immediately that's what she meant by *same*.

"Thanks for before. You saved me, and I didn't thank you—I'm sorry." She gave him a friendly smile, steeped in the charm boys her age would be hard-pressed to resist. Though it was a term not to be used easily around those who could manipulate magic, in a literary sense, one could say her appeal had magic hidden in it that would steal your heart away. —Well, in *popular* literary terms, anyway.

"In addition to thanking you, there's something I'd like to talk to you about... Do you have time to come with me for a little bit?"

Whether or not she was conscious of the effect her smile had on male high school students was up for debate, but she probably understood it quite well. Although, for Tatsuya, with his too-beautiful sister at his side, it might have been somewhat uncomfortable.

"I can't right now." Sayaka seemed more shocked than annoyed at his brief rejection, to which he followed up with, "Are you free in fifteen minutes?"

At Tatsuya's words, spoken quite definitively, she looked at him with a desolate, even blank expression, then hurriedly blinked a few times, and finally seemed to understand what she'd just been asked.

"Oh, yes, that works. I'll wait for you in the cafeteria." Though quite flustered at the unexpected response, she succeeded in obtaining Tatsuya's promise.

Tatsuya could only accompany his sister as far as the door of the student council room. Were he to enter, he'd probably see Hattori. Neither of them would be very comfortable if that happened, so Tatsuya, with nothing to do there anyway, had been naturally avoiding the student council room after school.

"All right, I'll be waiting for you in the library."

Until yesterday, Miyuki had always been waiting for Tatsuya. This was the first instance of him waiting for her, but it was the pattern he'd simulated in his head before school had started. He knew that she would surely come into some sort of official position. Therefore, he would not mistake how to spend his time. All the more because one of the reasons he'd come to this school in the first place was for the private literature and records he couldn't access except from organizations related to the National Magic University.

"The library?"

But Miyuki, who would have known all that, tilted her head and repeated what he'd said. Even he couldn't help but let doubt creep into his voice. "…That's my plan. Why?"

"No, it's just that you were going to go see Mibu in the cafeteria after this, so…" Miyuki's eyes were directed toward his collar.

"Miyuki?" Despite him saying her name, she didn't bring her face back up.

She didn't try to meet his gaze. In fact, she averted hers to the side.

Tatsuya didn't understand why his sister was acting this way. In anyone else's case she would have been sulking, but that was the one thing his sister would never do. Although he tried to get an answer out of her, the student council room was before their eyes and both were making people wait. "I don't think it's going to take very long. She probably just wants to recruit me for her club." He knew as well as anyone that was mistaken…but it gave him a chance to resolve the situation.

"…Is that really all it will be?"

"What?"

"Is it just a club recruitment offer? I think it might not be. I don't have a reason, but…I feel rather anxious. I'm very happy that you have won a reputation…but if they knew even a fraction of your real power, there would be many flocking to use you for their own ends. I think that those who wouldn't are in the minority. Please, take extra care."

It would have been easy to laugh it off as imaginary fears…if it hadn't been Miyuki Shiba saying it. "…Don't worry. I'll be fine no matter what happens."

"That's why I'm so worried!"

At last, Tatsuya got a dim idea of what his sister was afraid of. "…I'm all right. I would never get that desperate."

"…That's a promise, Tatsuya."

"All right… By the way, Miyuki, I don't think some committee activities in high school are enough to be called *winning a reputation*."

"…Geez! What does it matter, really? To me, your very name is famous, Tatsuya!"

Miyuki twirled herself around and headed for the card reader. Her cheek, hidden behind her black hair fluttering in an arc, was tinged with crimson.

He immediately found who he'd come here to meet—Sayaka was standing right near the entrance. "I wouldn't have minded if you'd sat down to wait."

"But then you might not have noticed, Shiba. I'm the one who invited you, so I didn't want to make you need to look."

It was a very feminine concern for him, or maybe it was just because she was older. But Tatsuya got the impression she didn't understand much about herself. She was sticking out like a sore thumb. He'd have to prepare himself for more annoying rumors after this. He sighed as the thought of the faces of two certain upperclassmen who would laugh mightily at his expense crossed his mind.

Of course, he wasn't careless enough to let his sigh show on the surface—on his face. He *was* meeting this girl for the first time, so it would be rude to sigh at her as soon as he met her. "In any case, let's sit down. Then we can talk."

"It's not very crowded, so we should buy drinks first." That was neither a question nor an invitation, but an assertion. He was a little surprised by it, but he wasn't about to suggest otherwise.

He bought coffee, and she juice; then they sat down at two empty seats, facing each other. He took a sip of his coffee, then, with the cup still in his hands, looked toward the opposite seat.

Sayaka focused on slurping up the brilliant scarlet liquid through a straw. She downed two-thirds of it in one go and finally looked back up.

Their eyes met.

She looked taken aback, and immediately reddened. It seemed very much like the hue of the juice had made its way into her face.

"...Do you like that kind of juice?" It was a plain question for Tatsuya, but...

"Mmgh... Who cares? I like sweet things! I'm basically just a child, after all!" ...She suddenly grew angry—no, sulky, even.

If it's so embarrassing, then why did you bother getting it? thought Tatsuya. He also felt that her degree of shyness and her level of defenselessness weren't in balance. But what he actually *said* was on a completely different vector. "I like sweet foods, too. I've never had that before, but I drink juice often at home."

"You do?"

"Yes."

"Oh..."

He didn't actually do anything of the sort, but Sayaka put a hand to her chest and sighed in relief. The action didn't make her look older than him—she seemed quite different from last week.

"Umm, well. Leaving all that aside... Again, thank you very much for last week. It was thanks to you the situation didn't get out of hand." She touched her knees together and placed her hands on them, straightened her posture, and gave a bow.

She was certainly the *kendo belle*—she seemed much more like that *now* than the "cute girl" she'd been until last week. He let his half-automatic observations flow toward the back of his mind and gave a noncommittal answer. "You don't need to thank me. I was doing my job."

Sayaka didn't seem satisfied with his formal reply, however. "I don't mean for just stopping Kirihara. That was a stupid duel we were having. Kirihara and I were one thing, but I wouldn't have been surprised if both the kendo club and the *kenjutsu* club were punished. It was resolved peacefully because you insisted there was no harm done, didn't you?"

"It really wasn't anything to make a big fuss about anyway. Aside from you and Kirihara, nobody was injured. After that it was just the *kenjutsu* club going nuts, so at the very least, the kendo club wouldn't be blamed for anything."

"But that's because you were fighting them—that's sort of why it wasn't a big problem. If it was anyone else, people would have gotten hurt for sure. Maybe other people could have stopped them without hurting them, but you dealt with so many of them without even letting yourself get hurt. I'm still in disbelief! I think the *kenjutsu* club should thank you for going easy on them.

"And about that, I *did* let Kirihara get hurt…so this might sound like an excuse or kind of unfeminine, but… If you do martial arts for a while, this kind of thing happens. The time comes, no matter what, when you can't hold back your desire to display your own strength in the process of achieving mastery. Shiba, you know what I mean?"

"I see—yes, I know."

—That was a lie. At least half of it, anyway. He didn't see his training as being martial arts. They were nothing more than combat techniques he was studying. He could understand the appeal of wanting to show off your ability to carry out your duty, but simply put, he had never had anything to do with impulses to simply flaunt his strength.

"Right?" However, Sayaka wouldn't have known much about what was deep inside him—obviously, since they'd only first talked to each other today. "No one needs to make a huge deal out of everything. Well, if people had been injured during that brawl, it would've probably been a big problem, but Kirihara was actually the only one who really got hurt. He and I were both fighting well aware we could get hurt, so it's nobody's business to make a fuss out of it."

That's wrong, thought Tatsuya. The problem was that Kirihara had broken the rules and used a highly dangerous spell. In principle, recruitment week troubles were handled within the club committee. If things would have ended with just Sayaka and Kirihara swinging their *shinai* around, Tatsuya would never have intervened, and Mari probably would have kept out of it, too.

Of course, he said none of this aloud.

"But there's still a lot of people who want to make such a small thing into a problem. A lot of students have been exposed for the same kind of thing—just so the disciplinary members could get better grades."

"...I am a member of the disciplinary committee at the moment, so...sorry."

"I-I'm sorry! I didn't mean it like that, really!" Feigning an ashamed expression, she looked at Tatsuya, who was bowing his head. Sayaka, suddenly flustered, began to explain herself in a mad haste. "What I wanted to say was that you're different from them, and that's why you helped me, and um, I didn't want to bad-mouth the disciplinary committee—well, I don't like them, but, umm...?"

Tatsuya expressionlessly observed Sayaka as her gestalt collapsed...though his own eyes were smiling. The random list of words she was saying had already lost all meaning, and they quickly faded out. Soon, he only saw her mouth opening and closing, with no sound coming out—and then she noticed the smirk in his gaze and looked down, embarrassed.

"...Hey, Shiba, you're kind of a bully..."

He felt like he'd heard that before. "I am not possessed of such a unique inclination," he said nonchalantly, pretending he didn't know what she meant. Then, forestalling any argument to the contrary, he continued. "So what did you want to talk about?"

"...I'll come right out and say it." Her lips were saying otherwise, but maybe she gave up or her sense of objective won out, because then she said, "Shiba, will you join the kendo club?"

Finally, she began to talk about the original reason he was here.

It was so predictable he couldn't deny feeling slightly deflated, but he already had an answer. *If she'd said that from the start, this would have gone more quickly,* he thought, a little irritated. He gave her his prepared reply. "I'm grateful for the offer, but I have to decline."

"…May I ask your reason?" Sayaka couldn't keep the shock out of her face at Tatsuya's immediate response, to which he didn't seem to have given even the slightest bit of thought.

"Actually, I'd like to ask why you invited me. My skills are empty-handed ones—they're completely different from kendo. With your level of skill, you know that, right?"

His tone was a calm one, not particularly rough or provocative, but there was an unmistakable sharp edge to what he'd actually said.

Sayaka's gaze wandered through empty space. She looked like she was desperately seeking an escape route. In a way, she probably was. After breathing a single sigh, she began to speak in an abstract way. "One's grades in magic are treated as the most important thing at Magic High School… I knew that much from the start, and still enrolled here. But don't you think it's wrong to decide everything just based on that?"

"Please, continue."

"There's no helping the fact that classes are separate. We just don't have any practical ability, that's all. But that's not all being at high school is supposed to be. Even clubs are prioritized based on magical talent, and that's wrong."

Just from what Tatsuya had seen this past week, there was no truth to the statement that clubs unrelated to magical competition were being unfairly oppressed by the school. It was true that the school provided various forms of support to competitive magic clubs. However, that was part of their advertising to make them look better as a magic high school, done from an administrative perspective.

In his view, this girl was making this fervent speech because she couldn't tell the difference between her not being given preferential treatment and her being given the cold shoulder.

However, that proved to be too hasty a conclusion. "I can't stand even my *sword skills* being scorned just because I can't use magic very well. I can't endure them being ignored. I won't let them deny everything I am just because of magic."

Her tone was unexpectedly strong. The emotion in it was beyond conviction, closer to deep-seated delusion—that's what Tatsuya felt.

Perhaps feeling uncomfortable at Tatsuya's steady, serious stare, Sayaka cleared her throat and repositioned herself. "The noncompetitive magic clubs have all decided to be allies. We got a lot of people who agree even from outside the kendo club. We're planning to create an organization separate from the club committee and announce our thoughts to the school at some point this year. I would like you to help as well, Shiba."

"I see…" He'd thought her more the idol type, but she was a true warrior woman. He smiled at how mistaken his impression had been.

"…Are you making fun of me?" It seemed she'd mistaken his smile.

He felt like leaving her misunderstanding alone would mean she wouldn't bother him in the future, but he went and said something he didn't need to anyway. "That's not what I meant. It was just funny how I thought wrong about you. I thought you were just a pretty girl who does kendo—I misjudged you…"

The second sentence was spoken half to himself. Ever since enrolling, there had been attractive girls appearing one after the other, each with one or two quirks. He actually felt like laughing loudly about having unconsciously hoped *this* one would be a normal, pretty girl.

"Pretty…" Perhaps because his awareness was directed inward at that time, Sayaka's mutter, her face flushing with red, and her suspicious fidgeting all passed him by.

"Mibu?"

"Wh-what is it?"

Still unaware of it, and suppressing an urge to smile, Tatsuya set his face again. Sayaka's voice in reply had been somewhat flustered, but he didn't show any signs of thinking about it. Then, he said something that was *really* unnecessary. "After you tell the school what you think, what are you going to do?"

"…Huh?"

[7]

The student council that day was quite different from how it used to be, and not even two weeks had passed.

First, the dining server had absolutely no part to play anymore. With Mari and Miyuki making their own lunches, Mayumi began to do so as well. With no past records, her skill made everyone a *little* anxious, though Mari was the only one actually worried. But she had gotten through the easier stages at a passable level, and now she was having fun changing up the kind of food she brought.

And there were more members now. Azusa usually ate with her classmates unless someone said something to her, but lately, people had been saying something every day. They invited her for a selfish reason, an absurd one—in any case, an illogical one: The ratio of freshmen to seniors in the room was unbalanced. Her personality wouldn't let her turn them down, though she'd probably accepted reluctantly.

On the other hand, the ratio of boys to girls was one to four. If *balance* was an issue, then this was a bigger one. They didn't seem to treat it as a problem.

"Tatsuya?"

"Yes, Chairwoman?"

In the middle of a lunch with those same members, Mari addressed him from across the table. (The positions at the table had Tatsuya seated next to Miyuki, with Mari across from him and Mayumi across from his sister, and Azusa next to Mayumi.)

Mari had tried to nonchalantly strike up a conversation, but there was no hiding the heckling in her smile. And even that expression looked good on her. "...Is it true you were *topping* Mibu, the sophomore, yesterday in the cafeteria? Conversationally, I mean."

Tatsuya was grateful he'd already finished eating. If something had been in his mouth, it would be everywhere right now. "...You're an adolescent lady, too, so I don't think you should use immodest terms like *topping*."

"Ha-ha-ha, thanks. You're about the only one who treats me like a lady, Tatsuya."

"Is that so? Your boyfriend must not be much of a gentleman if he doesn't treat his own girlfriend as a lady."

"That's not it! Shuu is—" Mari broke off and held her tongue, her expression implying she wished she hadn't said that.

"..." Tatsuya stared at his superior—well, the student who held a higher position in a high school committee, anyway—with an expression that was literally empty.

"..."

"..."

"...Why aren't you saying anything?"

"...Should I be making some sort of comment?"

Mari glimpsed bouncing, thick, wavy black hair out of the corner of her eye. Extremely reluctantly, she slid her gaze to the side.

And as expected...Mayumi had her back turned, and her shoulders were shaking. Mari gave her a pointed glare, then quickly looked away, returning her gaze to Tatsuya. "...So is it true you were topping Mibu from the kendo club?"

It looked like she wanted to treat all of that as though it hadn't happened. Tatsuya looked next to Mari; Mayumi stopped her stifled laughter and shrugged in an exaggerated manner.

—That was that, then. He decided to follow their house rules.

"Like I said, I don't think you should use terms like *topping*... I don't want you teaching such vulgar terms to my sister..."

"...Excuse me, Tatsuya? You *do* know how old I am, right...?" argued Miyuki reluctantly but modestly, her voice low. Tatsuya shot her a look of apology and immediately dropped it.

Once again, silence was the name of the battle. If this were a shogi match, the current player would be changing up their strategy.

But these house rules...meant that, unfortunately, it was Tatsuya who needed to change things up. "...That is not true."

"Oh, really? We have some witnesses who saw Mibu getting embarrassed, and her face getting bright red."

Tatsuya suddenly felt a chill drift over from the seat next to him.

"Tatsuya...? May I ask just what it was you were doing?"

It wasn't just his imagination; the temperature in the room was dropping physically and locally.

"M-magic...?" Azusa's mumble was tinged with fear.

Modern magic was the natural progression of supernatural ability research. Basically, modern magic, in an underlying sense, had succeeded the so-called characteristics of "supernatural abilities." The biggest difference between old magic and supernatural abilities was whether or not some non-thought process was required to activate it. This was the fundamental reason modern magic didn't absolutely *need* CADs, too.

At the same time, modern magic wasn't equivalent to supernatural abilities. Normally, espers could only use a certain type, or at most a few types, of strange powers. Modern magic had systematized and organized these so-called *supernatural abilities*. By introducing magic programs and activation programs, the tools for constructing magic programs, into the activation process, modern magic made it possible for people to use magic of dozens of types—even hundreds in some cases.

However, modern magic had a tendency to subdivide itself too thinly, and differing supernatural abilities that would be broadly measured under the same scale would end up in at *least* twenty or thirty different types. Despite that, modern magic was overwhelming in its versatility.

Modern users of magic, or magicians, used a plethora of magic through the medium of magic programs. The execution of magic used by these magicians, then, was adjusted to suit their own mental processes.

Magicians who were close to being espers and specialized in specific magic could activate magic through thought alone, without clear intent. Ones who used dozens of different types of magic, however, normally couldn't use magic accidentally.

It is true that magic programs are processed by the unconscious part of the mind, but that was only because the caster was making a deliberate choice. There was absolutely no chance they could formulate and execute magic programs wholly unintentionally.

If one of those magicians skilled in many types of magic could also activate their abilities unconsciously, that would be…

"That's quite impressive phenomenological influence…" murmured Mayumi. Tatsuya smiled drily. Even the now-abandoned supernatural abilities worked the same way to affect reality: by manipulating eidos, bodies of information that accompanied events. While magic running loose was proof of inexperience, it was also proof of superior talent.

"Calm down, Miyuki. I can explain. First restrain your magic."

"I'm so sorry…" Miyuki lowered her eyes out of embarrassment and slowly caught her breath. The room temperature stopped decreasing.

"Guess you don't need an air conditioner in the summer."

"Midsummer frostbite is nonsensical, though." Mayumi's joke seemed more to buy herself time to regain her own calm than to lighten the mood, but Tatsuya brushed it off. "It seems Mibu's inciting opposition among the students to the disciplinary committee's activities," he said, wrapping things up. Both Mari's and Mayumi's faces clouded. "But is it actually true that you get people in trouble on purpose for points? I know I didn't see anything like that—at least, not this week."

"I didn't, either. I could only look at where things happened over a monitor screen, but judging from how out of control it was, the actions taken by disciplinary officers actually seemed fairly tolerant."

At the siblings' suggestions, Mayumi's melancholic expression deepened. Mari shook her head and spoke. "Mibu is mistaken. Or maybe she's just biased. The disciplinary committee is a completely honorary post; there's no merit to being on it. Competition results might boost someone's seminar grades, but there's absolutely nothing like that here. You might gain some reputation just from being a member, but that doesn't even leave school walls. It's not like the student council, where being a member means you're seen highly even after graduating."

"...But it's also true that it has a lot of power at school," added Mayumi. "The disciplinary committee team actively maintains order here. If you were a student unhappy with how things are around here, they might look like a group of hound dogs abusing their power to you. Or, more accurately, someone is setting things up to make it *seem* like that."

Tatsuya couldn't help but be surprised. Things seemed to go a lot deeper than he realized. He asked the next natural question. "Do you know who it is?"

"Huh? Um, no, it's not really that easy to find the source of rumors, so..."

"...We could stop it if you found out who the culprit was, though."

For Mayumi and Mari, though, the question had been unexpected. Mayumi's remark had been a slip of the tongue. Tatsuya looked her dead in the eye—she immediately looked away. This was the first time he'd seen her so clearly disturbed. "I wasn't asking the identity of the underling at the end of things, spreading these false half-truths. I was asking about who's controlling things behind the scenes."

He felt his arm get tugged twice. He looked over to see Miyuki pulling at his sleeve, behind the table so others wouldn't see. She probably wanted to tell him he was overstepping his bounds, but Tatsuya didn't feel like backing down. His mind reproduced the image of the male student who'd attacked him with magic, then run away. He mentally zoomed in on the white wristband, its edges lined in red and blue, on the student's right wrist.

"An organization like Blanche, for example?"

Their unrest changed to shock. Mayumi and Mari both stiffened. Azusa watched them, her eyes wide; it didn't look like she'd been informed of the details.

"How do you know that name?"

"It's not like it's top secret information. There are apparently some press restrictions on it, but you can't suppress every little rumor that springs up."

For Tatsuya, the fact that Mayumi was *this* surprised was what surprised *him* more.

Blanche was an international anti-magic political organization. Their ideals were to oppose the current political system in which magicians were given special treatment by the government, as well as to eliminate societal discrimination based on magical ability.

But there was no truth to magic users being given special treatment by the government in this country in the first place. In fact, in reality, there was a *lot* of criticism of the government and the army for their inhumane treatment of magicians and of the way they used them as disposable tools. The country, though, couldn't avoid the necessity to make up the difference in the quantity of troops it could mobilize with quality, considering a certain neighboring country had the highest population in the world.

Military officers and administrative officials who were also magicians certainly received higher pay than those who were not, but that was no more than a reflection of how much work they needed to do.

It was no more than the price the nation paid for wearing down their souls with overwork.

Most anti-magic organizations conducted antiestablishment activities based on criticism of a reality they'd made up themselves. Among them, Blanche engaged in some of the most radical militant activities. This country supposedly protected freedom of political activity, so they were neither reined in nor oppressed. However, anti-establishment movements could gradually and easily slip into criminal acts—and in reality, there were multiple precedents of anti-magic groups conducting terrorist acts.

Currently, Blanche was representative of the kind of organization the public security bureau watched very closely.

And the color of the wristband worn by the student who had failed to dig out the ground beneath his feet was white, with one red edge and one blue edge—the symbol of a branch organization of Blanche called Égalité. The two organizations hid the fact that they were directly connected, but Égalité did actually operate under Blanche. The fact was, to those who knew, that they were no more then an outward-facing billboard for Blanche to attract youths fed up with the political situation.

They didn't know exactly how many people had become part of it. That student from before could possibly have been the first one. But the fact they had gotten not just a simple sympathizer, but one of their agents into the students likely meant they had secured a foothold at First High, otherwise it wouldn't have been possible.

"Trying to hide parts of it will only lead to bad outcomes, though... Oh, I'm not criticizing you, President, I'm just saying our government has managed this poorly."

Despite Tatsuya's consolation in the form of an excuse, Mayumi's expression didn't clear up. "...No, you're right, Tatsuya. It's true—there's a group that sees magicians as enemies. It would be better to spread correct information, including how unreasonable they are, than to hide their existence altogether along with the inconvenient agitation that seems so natural. We could be taking effective steps... but we're avoiding—no, running away from facing the problem."

She actually seemed like she was blaming herself. "You don't have much of a choice." His dismissive tone, therefore, came off as fairly cold. "This school is a national institution. We're just students, not government employees—at least, not yet. The student council is involved with operating the school; of course it would be held tight to the policies of the nation."

"Huh?" With a flat voice, unable to connect those words together in her head, Mayumi faltered for a moment, and Tatsuya looked at her.

"I mean that as the president, you had no choice but to keep it a secret," said Tatsuya, looking away from her uncomfortably.

Mari gave him a playful grin. "Wow, Tatsuya. You're pretty nice once in a while."

"But he's the one who put the president in that situation in the first place..." Azusa muttered blankly.

Mari immediately picked up for her. "Pressing someone like that and then supporting them, huh? The tactic of a gigolo. He managed to coax Mayumi, too. He's got skill!"

"W-wait, Mari, stop being weird!"

"Your face is red, Mayumi."

"Mari!"

The student council president and disciplinary committee chairwoman began to tease each other.

Tatsuya was looking in the wrong direction, his face feigning innocence—pretending not to notice his sister's cold stare upon him.

"All right... It's getting late, so we're going back to class. Let's go, Miyuki," said Tatsuya to Mayumi and Mari, still jostling each other, and rose from his seat.

Miyuki had been displeased, but he had brought her around with all sincerity, placating her. Azusa, who had watched it, had turned bright red and fled to the console in the corner of the room, but that was no concern of Tatsuya's.

"Oh, wait just one moment, Tatsuya," said Mari. "Okay, stop it, Mayumi, stop it already. We need to be serious now."

"...We will carefully deliberate upon this matter after school today."

"All right, all right... You're more tenacious than you look... Tatsuya, what is your answer going to be?"

"I'm the one waiting for an answer, so I'll decide once I hear it."

Sayaka had been unable to answer the question he'd posed to her yesterday in the cafeteria.

—After you tell the school what you think, what are you going to do?—

She just started making confused, unintelligible noises after that. She couldn't put together a response. So Tatsuya had given her some homework: He told her that when she figured it out, he'd listen to what she had to say again. "Based on what I just heard, this isn't something we can just let be."

"—I'll leave things to you."

"At this point, I can't even imagine *what* you're leaving for me to do."

"Whatever you can—I don't mind."

"How vague. Are you expecting something from me or not...? Well, if that's your condition, then I'll accept the task."

This wasn't something they could just let be—that wasn't just lip service. If the anti-magic organization was going to stop at just targeting the system itself, he didn't need to take the initiative. However, their antiestablishment activities were violent, steadily making targets out of individuals in symbolic positions. He couldn't discard the possibility that Miyuki would be targeted, since she had enrolled as the leading student and was now part of the student council. He was sure she would never lose out to some terrorists who could do nothing but skitter around in the shadows all day, but there was the worst-case scenario to think about.

"I'll do whatever I can," he said in acceptance, voice cool. He and Miyuki, who gave a small bow from behind him, went to the door and left the room.

Mari muttered to herself, "That's probably how we'll get the best outcome, after all."

Given how the disciplinary committee duty worked, Tatsuya didn't need to show up to the headquarters every day. Even the chairwoman normally hung around the student council room upstairs. The members elected to it were all the cream of the crop, each violent and uncompromising. Such people tended to neglect clerical work and tidiness, so because no one stayed there for very long, the room had been left to utter dilapidation.

Before Tatsuya's achievements during the club recruitment week, he had—reluctantly—established a firm position as the one person in the disciplinary committee with any clerical skills. So, despite not actually being on duty, he'd gotten a call for help from Mari regarding the activity reports of the club recruitment week, that oh-so-bloody battlefield. They hadn't been organized in the slightest…though it wasn't so much *help* as Tatsuya just doing it all himself.

It had not been his intention to fall into this situation. His plan, at the time of his enrollment, had been to use his after-school time to browse the private, university-owned research documents and materials that you could only view with specific terminals in the National Magic University and the magic high schools affiliated with it. And yet here he was, doing this and that, going here and there, getting none of his research done.

I suppose I'll finish up these incident reports… he figured to himself with a sigh, knowing how unproductive it was. First he needed to meet up with Miyuki, so he went to log out of a terminal, having completed a different task—and just then, something happened.

A notification appeared on the display that he'd received an e-mail. The timing was too perfect. The school's crest was attached to it. That meant it contained instructions that a student wouldn't be able to refuse, or an official notification e-mail. He couldn't just ignore something like that. He hadn't gotten far up out of his seat, but he sat back down and opened it up.

Displayed in the "sender" field was the name Haruka Ono.

"Sorry for calling you out so suddenly!"

"It's all right, ma'am. I didn't have anything urgent to do."

They were in the counseling room. Haruka had given the standard apology, her smile not showing any regret at all; Tatsuya had given the proper response to it, not really meaning it.

In truth, he found this summoning to be a pain. He wasn't in a hurry, but he *had* promised to help Mari. Sending an e-mail to notify her wouldn't have been enough, so after apologizing to her profusely over voice communication, he ended up getting even more work to do than he'd planned.

He'd had to cancel walking Miyuki home, too. She seemed unaffected on the surface, but he'd already gotten a headache thinking of how he'd try to improve her mood when they got back to their house. Besides, he had nothing he wanted to talk to a counselor about anyway.

"So have you gotten used to the high school life?" asked Haruka, popping a standard question, whether or not she knew of his actual feelings on the matter (he was pretty sure she didn't).

Tatsuya's answer, though, was far from standard. "No, ma'am."

"...Is there something worrying you?"

"I have a lot more to do than I thought I would, and it's hard to focus on my studies, ma'am." On the supplementary sound channel he was telling her that she was wasting time, and to quit the small talk and get to what she needed to say.

Even if she didn't hear any of that nuance, she seemed to still understand that he wasn't in a very amicable mood. She gave a vague smile, somewhere between a dry grin and a friendly one, then made a display of recrossing her legs.

He got a glimpse of her sensual thighs covered in thin stockings from under her short, tight skirt. There was nothing to obstruct their gaze between the chairs they sat facing each other in.

Modern etiquette discouraged the exposure of skin in public places. Female students were no exception—they all wore thick, opaque tights or leggings under their skirts. That was the school's policy. Even leaving aside how mature the girl was, this was a stimulating sight he didn't see very often at all. (Incidentally, even those styles that didn't show any skin at all could be worn comfortably during the summertime, thanks to advancements in fiber materials.)

"…What's wrong?" asked Haruka playfully to Tatsuya, who was unconsciously staring and unable to peel his eyes away.

He quickly averted his stare and would have given a disordered response—"Going by the present dress code…"—but Tatsuya's answer was a tad different from the norm. "…I believe your outfit is too stimulating, Ms. Ono."

"I-I'm sorry!"

There was no arousal in his eyes—in fact, they seemed cold and observing, and his tone gave the impression of a light criticism. Haruka, flustered, got her legs into a more modest position and sank back into her seat.

Inducing unrest in someone was the universal technique for taking the initiative. Haruka had chosen this kind of clothing to that end. But this freshman (Tatsuya) would only reply with an expressionless gaze.

She couldn't figure him out. She was unable to gain the initiative, and it confused her.

"In any case, why have you called me here?" Despite trying to clamp down on it, his voice betrayed a tiny bit of irritation. And it was doubtful even *that* wasn't part of his own act.

He might have been going on just sixteen years old, but she wasn't trying to make light of him. She knew normal means wouldn't work against him, and that's exactly why she'd attempted to use sex appeal, a method she wasn't used to. Unfortunately for her, it looked like she had to give up on that safe, roundabout plan.

Having made up her mind, she once again faced Tatsuya. "I came here to request your assistance, Shiba, with our work."

"*Our* work, ma'am?"

She knew of his intelligence, even if only from the entrance exam. Nevertheless, his reply went straight for the vitals, putting her more and more on guard. "Yes—the counselors'." She had the brief sense that he was seeing right through her. Right now, though, her only option was to keep pushing with her "counselor work" charade. "The tendencies of students tend to change by the year. For example—you use *ma'am* and *sir* quite frequently, don't you? It wasn't too unusual to hear while such a percentage of students in magic high schools desired military posts, but common use of those terms first spread among the other students after our victory three years ago at the Defense of Okinawa. Changes in the social climate bring about changes in student mentality as well. Especially after a big incident's happened—the ways they think and feel about things and themselves change to the point where you couldn't believe they were all the same age."

She paused for a moment, gauging the boy's expression. He didn't seem disturbed in the slightest. In fact, he seemed like he was listening to things he was already aware of. "So every year, we pick around ten percent of the new students and have them undergo continued counseling. It's so that we can get a good grasp of the student mentality each year and conduct the best counseling we can."

"I would be a guinea pig, in other words, ma'am?" His words easily summed it up. She didn't sense any of the negative emotions that he should have shown, like anger, indignity, or distaste. "If that's all it's for, then I'll assist you, ma'am—but what is your real objective?" he replied with a faint smile.

At that moment, Haruka needed to use all her might to suppress her bewilderment. "...Do you think I'm concealing my real objective? That's upsetting. I'm not a harpy, you know." Her tone was light and jocular to the last—and was more to keep him from realizing she'd lost her calm than to placate him.

"I believe I'm a bit too unique to use as a sample, ma'am."

"I see. I'm of the same impression—that you're not quite a normal freshman. That's why I want you to help us, though. You might be the first instance of someone breaching the walls between Course 1 and Course 2 students, but that doesn't mean you'll be the last."

"...I'll accept that, then, ma'am."

Haruka was relieved—it seemed like she'd talked him down for the moment. He didn't seem *completely* convinced, but unraveling stubborn minds like his was where counselors displayed their skill, she told herself. —Ignoring reality somewhat, that is.

"I regret making you feel like you can't trust me because of my inexperience, Shiba... In any case, may I ask you a few questions?"

"Yes, go ahead, ma'am."

She knew he was being cautious of her, but they didn't have all the time in the world here. In order, she presented the questions she'd prepared beforehand to Tatsuya.

Counseling was a profession to which privacy was crucial. Protecting the confidentiality of clients was the cornerstone of their professional ethical code. That meant when faced with someone confiding in them, they would ask the person questions in order to solve their issue and never leak any of that to a third party—but in this situation, where Haruka was the one to ask *him* for help, she wouldn't be able to set foot into his private life. Consequently, the topic of her questions was limited to what had happened at school since his first day.

And after Haruka had finished listening to Tatsuya himself briefly talk about the troubles he'd had since starting school, this was her reaction:

"...Thanks. I'm surprised you're still okay. With that kind of stress accumulating, it wouldn't be odd for a person to have a mental breakdown," she said in some admiration, her expression doctorial.

She actually had a medical license, and she specialized in mental health—that's why Tatsuya would call her a "doctor," but he thought she was listening to what he had to say as a counselor.

"From a medical standpoint, you might be right, ma'am. Exceptions spring up in any aggregate data set, though."

At Tatsuya's remark that clinical data was always a by-product of statistical processing, Haruka looked away in embarrassment.

Her eyes wandered for a few moments, but she then noticed Tatsuya glancing at the old-fashioned (read: *behind-the-times*) wall clock—he was doing it so that she would notice, of course—and quickly looked back at him. "Right, that was all I wanted to ask for today... By the way, may I ask you one thing that isn't directly related to counseling?"

"What is it, ma'am?"

"Is it true that Mibu, the sophomore, asked you out?"

"...That really doesn't have anything to do with counseling," said Tatsuya, not bothering to hide his amazement.

Haruka hurriedly continued. "If it was Mibu, I would have an interest... I can't talk about the specifics, though."

"It would be a problem if I heard about things private to others. Just where on earth did you hear such a groundless accusation?"

"Groundless...?"

"Yes, ma'am—is there something wrong?"

"No, it's nothing... Well, truthfully speaking, if you had been of the mind to start dating her, there was something I wanted to ask of you. But if that isn't how you feel, then don't worry about it."

"I already said all the nonsense about her asking me out was groundless, ma'am. Anyway, where did you hear about that?"

She purposely averted her eyes from his at his repeated question. "I'm sorry—it's a confidential matter."

He didn't pursue the point any further. "Then I will get going now, ma'am." Instead, he got up and headed for the exit, not waiting for a reply.

"If there's anything bothering you about Mibu, you can talk to me anytime."

There was something like conviction in Haruka's voice as she spoke to his back—a conviction that something that *would* bother him would happen. Tatsuya had no interest in what that might be, but he also didn't stop and turn around. He didn't have the sort of innocent charm to let a pointless curiosity lead him into a trap.

After dinner, as Tatsuya was in his bedroom at his console, a voice came to him from the other side of the door.

"Tatsuya, it's Miyuki."

Practically speaking, Tatsuya and Miyuki were the only ones who lived in this house. It was plain as day who would have been knocking at his door without her needing to name herself, and he didn't need a name if he heard her voice, either.

Still, though, at every turn, Miyuki always announced herself like this. As though trying to imprint her name into Tatsuya's mind. As though she were afraid he might forget it.

"You can come in," prompted Tatsuya without looking away from the display. From the door, the console was embedded in the side wall. As he read through lines of text, scrolling at high speed, he glimpsed the figure of his sister in his peripheral vision.

"The cake you bought for us has arrived… Shall we have some tea?" There was hesitation in her invitation—probably out of a sense that she didn't deserve her brother's needless consideration in this particular case.

For Tatsuya, if a cake was all it took, it was a small price to pay—but her modesty was another one of his sister's charms. —Not that just anyone could bring it out of her, though.

The cake has arrived was a phrase that would have been quite limited in usage a hundred years ago, but the expression was used on a daily basis in today's world. Advances in physical distribution systems had turned the term *baggage* into a dead word. You could get even small things like cakes delivered for free. Of course, for the stores, creating and shipping the product upon receiving the order had two merits: not needing to keep extra goods in storage, and the turnover rate of customers. The service was weighed upon a scale of minimized shipping costs.

"I'll be right there," he answered, saving the displayed information into their home network's shared directory.

Tatsuya's washed down the not-too-sweet cream left in his mouth from the chocolate cake—Miyuki's favorite—with coffee he'd had her make more bitter than usual, then switched the living room's display to data-viewing mode.

"...Is it all right if I see this as well?"

Tatsuya hadn't finished eating either or anything, and Miyuki was going at an even slower pace. Nevertheless, his calling up a data file clearly meant that he wanted to show something to her. "Of course," he said. Despite that, she had still asked for confirmation first, and upon his affirmative reply, she settled back into her seat. "It may not be a topic suited to family entertainment, but it seems like you're not going to avoid getting tangled up in this, so I figured we should share information sooner rather than later... No, it's nothing to sit at attention for." His sister had put down her fork and sat up straight, and he waved away the action as unnecessary. He gave her a dry grin, which she answered with a slightly embarrassed one, and picked up her fork again.

"Open cabinet name *Blanche*."

He couldn't bring a full keyboard out onto the living room table with all the food laid out. Tatsuya didn't like it very much, but he used voice commands to bring up the files containing his findings one by one on the display.

"That's the anti-magic activist political society that came up during lunch, right?"

"They call themselves a civic movement, though. Behind the scenes they're a prime example of a terrorist group. And there doesn't seem to be any doubt these *terrorists* are moving around in the shadows at school. There is a group called Égalité—a branch organization of Blanche—and during my activities as disciplinary committee officer, I actually saw a student who I believed to be part of it."

Tatsuya's words caused Miyuki surprise, and she cocked her head to the side. "At Magic High School—a student of Magic High School?"

"I can understand why you'd find it hard to believe," nodded Tatsuya deeply, indicating that he empathized with her bewilderment. "People who believe that magic high schools, not just First High, will help them with their magic are all coming to study magic. Whether it's for their own sake or for another's is a separate issue. A student of a magic high school rejecting magic is no more than a self-contradiction."

It was a perfect and complete contradiction, and that was all. For Tatsuya, magic in the eyes of society labeled him negatively in some respects, but as someone who studied and researched magic, he didn't feel like he wanted to reject it.

"It's obviously strange when you think about it… But the obvious doesn't work, so the strange people run rampant."

"…Why is it like that, I wonder?"

"If you try to think about it using normal logic, you'll get trapped in a maze. So instead of thinking about it logically, you have to think about it on a concrete, individual level. The first point that needs to be addressed is that despite them waving their flags of anti-magic beliefs in the air, they don't outwardly reject magic."

"Come to think of it…that's true."

"Their aim is abolition of the societal discrimination due to magic. That in itself is undeniably correct."

"…Right."

"What is discrimination, then?"

"When society's opinion of someone doesn't reflect their actual skills and hard work…?"

"Like I said, Miyuki, you shouldn't think about it from a general viewpoint." As he spoke, he smoothly picked up the remote control on the sideboard, then pointed it at the screen. One of the areas of the sixteen-way split screen came to the front and magnified. "Blanche, in terms of its outward political society guise, cites the difference in average salary earned by magicians and non-magician company workers as proof that magicians are being given special treatment. The discrimination they're talking about, in the end, is a difference in average pay. But they're only talking about averages, about results. They don't think at all about how exhausting and taxing the work done by highly paid magicians is. They also completely ignore the vast number of 'spare' magicians who, despite having magical skill, can't get employed in occupations related to magic, and actually make less money on average."

The emotion in his flat voice was sparse, but there was just a hint of downheartedness in it. "No matter how strong it may be, magic that society doesn't value won't bring either money or honor."

Miyuki cast her gaze downward, bitterly. He got up, walked around her, and gently put a hand on her shoulder. "The reason the average magician's salary is high is because there are ones who do possess rare skills that society needs. Among those scant few magicians, there are a relatively high percentage of top earners, which means the average salary is calculated as being high, that's all. And those magicians working at the forefront contribute to society—actually, that's too pretty a way of putting it. Magicians receive high rewards for creating some sort of profit, whether it's financial or not; but they aren't given special treatment in a financial sense just because they're magicians. Their world is not an easy one—they can't live in luxury just by having the innate talent for magic. We know that all too well. Don't we, Miyuki?"

"Yes... I know it well," said Miyuki, nodding deeply and placing her own hand atop her brother's on her shoulder.

"What this essentially means is that Blanche's stance of opposition to magic-based discrimination really means they're opposed to magicians being paid in a financial sense. They want magicians to donate their services to society unselfishly."

"...I believe that a rather selfish, arrogant thing for them to say. Magicians and non-magicians are alike in that they need money to live. And yet they say they can't allow magicians to make a living with magic, and that those who can use it have to make a living on something else... Doesn't that just mean they're saying they don't want to respect magic as a human skill because they can't use it themselves? They're saying magicians don't need to be repaid for the effort they put into studying magic, and that their hard work shouldn't logically need to be respected... Or are those kinds of people not aware that you can't use magic with natural, inborn talent alone? Has nobody told them that using magic requires long years of learning and training?"

Tatsuya pulled away from Miyuki's back, gave a cynical smile, and returned to his seat. "No, they know. They just don't mention it. It would be too inconvenient to say it, to think it. The ideal of *equality* is easy on the ears, so they trick others with it—and themselves. Remember what you asked at the beginning? About why students in a magic high school would be active in anti-magic groups like Blanche and Égalité?"

"Yes... You mean they don't understand what the magic-rejecting faction really wants...?"

"People who can't learn to use magic, no matter how hard they try, think it's unfair that those who can use it to gain high positions. Then, even if you can use magic, the students with less talent for it think that it's strange they can't catch up to those with abundant talent even though they put in a lot of work, and that it's strange they should be seen as inferior... It wouldn't be mysterious to think this way, would it? Differences in talent aren't limited to magic—it happens in every single field in every kind of human work. Even if you don't have magical talent, you might have other talent. If you can't stand not having magical talent, then you should find a different way of life."

For those who didn't know any more about Tatsuya than what he showed, it would have sounded like he was saying that for his own benefit. But Miyuki, the only person here listening to him, wasn't prone to such a misunderstanding.

"The only reason for those studying magic to reject magical 'discrimination,' I think, is because they can't get away from magic. They don't want to leave it, but they can't stand not being seen as a full-fledged magician. They can't stand the fact that the same amount of effort on their part won't make them catch up. They can't stand the possibility that even working many times as hard won't make them catch up either. So they reject being judged based on magic. Of course, they're aware that those with the talent are paying the full price in hard work. They see it personally, every day. But they look away from the truth, shove all the responsibility onto 'inborn magical talent,' and reject it. Well... It isn't as though I *can't* understand such weakness. I have similar feelings as well."

"That's not true!" Miyuki knew as well as he did that he wasn't seriously deprecating himself. But she still couldn't help but protest. "You have a kind of talent nobody else can emulate, Tatsuya! Just because you don't have the same talents as everyone else... You've done many-times-harder work to come this far, haven't you?!"

Tatsuya didn't have normal talent, that was all—he had a magical talent *far exceeding others*. Miyuki was proud of being the one who best understood that. If anyone was trying to deny that, even if it was the person himself, her older brother, she couldn't let that slide.

"That's because I had a different talent."

"Ah..." Tatsuya, however, had still said he could "understand such weakness" even in understanding of what Miyuki was trying to say. She realized her refutation had been shortsighted, and her cheeks flushed crimson with embarrassment.

"I covered for my lack of talent in modern magic with another talent. I can comment from an objective viewpoint like this *because* I had that option. If I hadn't...I might have been clinging to the beautiful ideal of *equality* myself. Even if I knew it was a lie."

"..."

She didn't argue with her brother's matter-of-fact tone this time. Miyuki already knew what he was trying to say. Tatsuya was neither lamenting himself nor pitying others; he was talking about the "human weakness" that existed in him, too.

"Those with inferior magic talent don't want to think about the fact that it's inferior, and so they preach the ideal of equality. Those who can't use it at all don't want to think about the fact that it's just another type of talent people can have, and so they veil their jealousy with ideals. So then, what about those who understand all of that, and are still fanning the flames? The equality they talk about is to treat everyone the same whether or not they can use magic. The abolition of societal discrimination based on magic is the same as not valuing magical skills. And when it comes down to it, that's a denial of the significance of magic in society. Magic cannot advance in a society that does not value it. Hidden behind those who shout their opposition to magic discrimination and those who scream for equality between magicians and non-magicians is a faction that wishes to make this country abandon magic."

"What is this faction...?"

"For better or worse, magic is power. Money is power, too, and technology, and the military. Magic has the potential to be the same kind of power as battleships and fighter jets. Military uses for magic are being researched all over the world, in fact, and plenty of military spies are hard at work snooping around through magic technology."

"Then the magic-denying faction's objective is for this country to abandon magic, and thus cause the nation to lose its power?"

"Probably. And because of that, they'll spare no efforts—even inhuman terrorism. With that said, who is it that would benefit from this nation losing power?"

"Wait... Then they'd be supported by..."

"That's right. And the Ten Master Clans would never leave *them* unchecked. Especially not the Yotsuba family. So we need to take extra care while we still have the chance."

He didn't say what they should be cautious *of.* There was no need to say it between the two of them.

Miyuki nodded to her brother, her face slightly pale.

[8]

With the club recruitment (war?) week ending, enrollment-related events came to a close.

Even Tatsuya's class got up to full tilt with its magic studies.

Serious, focused education in magic began in the high school curriculum, but given the fact that the entrance exams included a practical portion, the students had already acquired some fundamental magical skills by the time they enrolled.

Classes were conducted based on this, too—so even though one would systematically relearn everything from the start, there were cases of students who were poor at practical abilities becoming unable to keep up not long after school started.

From a certain point of view, the Course 1/Course 2 divide was logical for taking this gap into consideration so that neither would negatively affect the other—even if that *was* leaving one side behind.

"Nine hundred and forty milliseconds. Tatsuya, you did it!"

"Sheesh... Third time's the charm, I guess."

Mizuki's eyes glittered in vicarious pleasure, and Tatsuya responded with a tired grin.

Their class was in the middle of magical practice.

It involved pairing up, then compiling and executing a single type of magic program under a time limit.

One would read in an activation program, then use it as a base and let their magic calculation region, an unconscious region of the magician's brain, construct and execute a magic program.

That was the modern system of magic.

Under this scheme, the process of converting the activation program—data that could be stored on a device—into a magic program that could not, used the word *compile*, which was taken from information technology parlance.

In modern magic, the scheme of digitizing the necessary work to execute magic and converting that data into an activation program, then using that as a base to construct a magic program, meant that it was accurate, safe, and versatile.

In exchange for that, it sacrificed the speed possessed by supernatural abilities, wherein a person could alter events just by willing it. As it placed the extra step of constructing a magic program in the middle, there was nothing that could be done about it. However, while the construction time for magic programs couldn't be reduced to zero, you could come infinitely close to it.

The reason modern magic placed an emphasis on the speed at which one constructed magic programs went something like this: CADs were originally only a storage device meant to record the original activation program data, but magic execution speed quickly became the main point. The CAD they were using in class today didn't need to be adjusted based on each individual—and because of that, there were absolutely no functions that supported speeding it up. The goal of today's practice was to practice compilation speed by using this CAD, which was, in a certain sense, the way the devices were originally.

If one member of the pair couldn't clear it, the other would automatically be kept for overtime. Mizuki had completed it on her first try, so for Tatsuya, this was the time to breathe a sigh of relief.

"But I was a little surprised. You really are bad at using magic practically, aren't you?"

For single-type, single-process spells like the one they were using, the aim for magicians was to get the time between starting to read in a completely expanded activation program and executing the magic down to less than five hundred milliseconds.

Tatsuya, who needed three attempts to get under just one thousand milliseconds, couldn't be called *positive* even in flattery. "Surprising? I feel like I make that assertion a lot."

"I do hear you say it quite often...but I assumed you were just being modest. I mean, you can do anything, Tatsuya. I didn't think you'd be bad at actually using magic."

Mizuki tilted her head to the side, utterly confused, and Tatsuya couldn't keep a dry grin from his face—he didn't have the option to choose any other expression. "...It might sound like I'm bragging, but if my practical skills were average, I wouldn't have been in this class at all."

He took particular care not to let his tone sound sarcastic at all. Perhaps it worked—or maybe she was just being considerate—since she nodded straightforwardly. "I see. If you were good at practical skills, too...you'd be a little perfect! We might not have wanted to come near you," said Mizuki, giving a carefree smile.

He was smiling along with her, but it got to him a little.

"But Tatsuya... Don't you get frustrated?"

"...With what?" He couldn't figure out what her repeated expression of confusion meant, so he started to want to answer her question.

"You're actually very skilled, but you're seen as having no talent. I think normal people would be frustrated. I personally can't help feeling frustrated. If I had the kind of skill you do, I don't think I'd be able to endure being looked down on as a Weed...but you don't seem to care about it much, so..."

It was an extremely difficult-to-answer question.

Given Mizuki's personality, he didn't think she'd go and spread mean rumors or tell others, but if he were to try and give a convincing response, he'd need to get somewhat into his own personal circumstances. "Processing speed is a form of skill—and an important factor, at that. There are plenty of times where a tenth of a second can mean the difference between life and death. They're not wrong in thinking I don't have talent."

Tatsuya decided to choose the answer he *could* say in public.

If Mizuki had been just any Course 2 student, she probably would have been satisfied with that.

But she—"But in the real world, Tatsuya, you can activate magic a lot faster, can't you?"—was possessed of special "eyes."

"…Why do you think that?" He knew giving such a response itself meant that he was admitting to what she'd said, and that he had been defeated, but amid his confusion he could produce no better reply.

"During that practice, you looked like you were having a really hard time on all three attempts. My mom is a translator, so it might sound strange, but it's like you're a person who can think about an English question in English and answer in English, but it wants to force you to answer in Japanese first and then translate it to English. And during the first attempt, you had almost put together a magic program, but then you got rid of it and redid the compile, didn't you? From a timing point of view, you were reading in the activation program and constructing the magic program in parallel. And that's when it hit me—that maybe you didn't *need* to use an activation program for this level of magic. Maybe you could just construct a magic program directly."

Using magic with the same speed as this, but without using an activation program—in other words, not using a CAD. He was under strict command to keep this skill a secret.

And she'd seen through it with just one attempt.

The very core of his mind froze over.

His caution reached its peak, his confusion went past its limit, and then subsided as he regained his calm.

Tatsuya was not at all used to being shaken like that; it was a very rare experience for him.

"I didn't think you had seen that far. You really do have a good pair of eyes."

This time, Mizuki's face was the one that paled, reaffirming Tatsuya's belief that she'd been trying to keep her own "eyes" a secret.

Maybe that was a little mean, he thought, the corners of his mouth turning up just slightly. But judging from her reaction, there was now far less risk of her seeing through to the true essence of this secret skill he had.

He then decided to give her one more push. She already knew that he was able to call forth magic programs without using an activation program. So by leading her to think it was purely a skill achieved through personal effort, he could lead her interest away from it. If he satisfied her curiosity just the right amount, then, considering her personality, she wouldn't dig any deeper. "You're right—if it's a single type of spell, I can execute a little faster by creating a magic program directly. But I can only use it for magic that doesn't involve a whole lot. Five processes is as high as I can go."

The term *process* in the context of modern magic referred to two things: One was the actual process of executing magic, and the other was each individual step of activating multiple spells that you would put together to achieve some desired alteration in events. When Tatsuya referred to five processes, he meant a technique that brought forth a single event alteration by using five different "pieces" of magic put together.

For example, if you were going to use magic to move an egg from the kitchen to the table, you would need four processes: acceleration, movement, deceleration (negative acceleration), and stopping (ceasing movement).

Movement magic overwrote the speed of an object and its linear coordinates; if you didn't also apply a specific acceleration process, the movement would ignore the target's inertia and accelerate it. In the case of an egg, it would crack.

If you eliminated the movement process and tried to only use acceleration and deceleration, the egg would end up moving along a projectile path, and you'd need *extremely* precise deceleration control. It was easier, even at the cost of additional processing, to apply deceleration at the same rate as acceleration, then bring its speed to zero with a movement spell.

In contrast, man-to-man combat magic that launched your opponent was completed with just movement magic—one process. The objective was to damage the opponent in the first place, so there was no need for an extra process to soften the impact.

"I'd think five would be more than enough to use in combat..."

In general, consumer-use magic required more layers of processing than did combat-use magic. As Mizuki said, one- to five-process magic would probably cover the majority of combat spells.

"It's not like I'm not studying magic for combat, though. I still need activation programs to get the most out of spells with more than one step, and I'm slower than others at doing that, so I'm naturally seen as inferior—which is fine," he said, giving another thin smile. For some reason, though, Mizuki looked up at him with a film over her eyes. For a moment, Tatsuya got a terrible feeling—had he made a fatal mistake somewhere? But that calculation error itself was quickly shown to have been a mistaken result.

"That's amazing, Tatsuya... I really respect that!" she said, fascinated, folding her hands in front of her. For Tatsuya, anyway, she had just said something he couldn't ignore.

"Huh?"

"Normally people want to be magicians because they can use magic...but you actually have a real goal in mind for studying it..."

"Um, well, that's true, but..."

"I must mend my ways!"

"Err..."

"I was really only studying magic to learn how to control my eyes, and I've never really given much thought to what I want to use magic for in the future, but from now on, I'll be certain to think about it!"

What? She…she wasn't trying to keep the stuff about her eyes a secret? thought Tatsuya at last, but he couldn't get a word in edgewise because her energy was overwhelming him. "Hello? Miss Mizuki?"

"I see, I get it. If you have a clear objective, then of course you wouldn't fall apart just because someone spoke badly about you. If you can achieve goals that are important to your life, then your grades in school are really just secondary! That's what makes it worth living. Everyone lives their lives searching for meaning—"

"Hey, Mizuki, what are you all excited for?"

Mizuki's solo recital—during the middle of class—continued until Erika cut in.

At last, Mizuki noticed the strange stares of her classmates—or the blank stares, really—and blushed and looked down.

As he watched her do so, he kept his expression discreet so as not to let his cynicism show on his face.

Meaning of life? That was far more than what it was. He never had the option of living a life without magic. He wasn't going to become a magician because he could use magic. He had been made into a magician despite being unable to use magic.

Magic had been a curse for him ever since the moment he was born. All he was doing was struggling to change it into something he could tolerate.

But… If it was normal to become a magician if you could use magic, then it wouldn't be odd in the slightest for magicians in the making to reject magic.

And then he thought…that maybe, just maybe, he'd made a slight error in his thinking.

And then, at lunch break, Tatsuya ended up staying behind anyway… because Erika and Leo begged him to.

"A thousand and sixty milliseconds… Keep it up. Just a little more."

"I-it's so far away... I had no idea point-one seconds could be so far away..."

"You don't say time is *far away*, stupid. It's *long*."

"Erika... You got a thousand and fifty-two milliseconds."

"Ahhhhh! Stop it! I was making fun of him to take a break!"

"I-I'm sorry..."

"No, it's okay, Mizuki. Gotta face reality, no matter how harsh it is to you..."

"...I don't give a damn about this stupid play thing you're doing! Stop treating people like toys!"

Erika and Leo had been cooperating to fail at the exercise ever since class was in session, so they'd asked Tatsuya to coach them.

"Leo, you're taking too long to take aim. You're not trying to be a perfect marksman, here."

"Yeah, I know, but..." Leo, who no longer had the energy to hide his complaints, nodded in agreement.

"Well, I suppose you do... Well, guess I'll share a trick with you—what if you aim it first, then read in the activation program?"

"Wait, you can do that?"

"Yeah, but it's a trick. It's not practical, and it would only work here, so I don't really want to teach you how..."

"What? Please, Tatsuya! I don't care if it's a trick or a cheat or whatever, just tell me!"

Leo put his hands together over his head and begged. Tatsuya sighed. "Don't put words in my mouth. It's not against the rules or anything... Geez, and I've been saying how bad I am at application this whole time, too. If you want to learn, you should ask someone with *actual* skill."

"You say you're bad at it, but you're better than me! And you even know how compilation works on the inside. You're the only one pointing out what I'm doing wrong, too."

"I said I'll teach you—no need to flatter me... And as for Erika..."

"What could it be? I don't care if it's a cheat or against the rules or whatever, please tell me! My stomach is growling!"

"I said, stop putting words in my mouth! Uhh, right, as for you... I don't know what the issue is."

"Whaaaat?"

"Frankly, I don't understand why you can't do this. You're compiling far smoother than I was."

"No way! Don't abandon me, Tatsuya!"

Teary-eyed—probably as an act—she put her fingers together and looked up at him, clinging to him with her gaze. He sighed again.

The two of them act the exact same way, he thought. But he said something else. "Well, how about this? Erika, when you're reading in the activation program, try putting your hands on top of each other on the panel."

"Huh?" At that, Erika—and Mizuki as well—gave him blank stares. "...That's it?"

"I'm not confident or anything, so if it works out, I'll explain why."

"O-okay... I'll give it a shot."

After Tatsuya saw her put her doubts to the side for the moment and face the stationary CAD, he started to lecture Leo on the "trick."

Excess psionic light glimmered, and numbers other than the time were displayed on the top part of the small, round target. It was a scale attached to the target, showing the maximum pressure applied by the single weighting-type spell. It was set up so that it would record the time it took to actually activate when the scale detected a certain amount of force.

"One thousand ten milliseconds. Erika, you went down forty milliseconds all at once! Just one more push and you'll have it!"

"O-okay, I got this! I feel like I can do this now!"

"One thousand sixteen. Don't hesitate, Leo. You know where the target is. You don't need to bother looking at it."

"G-got it. Next time for sure!"

As Tatsuya and Mizuki reset the measure, Erika and Leo closed their eyes, stretched their arms, and focused their minds, each in their own way, to get ready to try again.

Then, from behind Tatsuya came a reserved voice.

"Tatsuya, may I be so rude as to interrupt...?"

He knew the voice belonged to his sister without needing to turn around.

Erika, though, did turn around at the multiple pairs of footsteps. "Miyuki... Oh, and Mitsui and Kitayama, right?"

"Erika, don't lose focus," chided Tatsuya. "Sorry, Miyuki. One more and we'll be good, so just wait a minute."

"Eh?"

"I understand. I truly apologize, Tatsuya."

Miyuki smiled and gave a slight bow when Tatsuya turned around and apologized.

Leo grimaced at the nonchalant pressure that had been placed on him. Tatsuya nodded his head to him. "Okay, this is the moment of truth."

He hadn't raised his voice, but his tone had been peremptory.

"Right!"

"Okay! This is it!"

The two of them, brimming with spirit, turned toward the CAD panel.

"We're finally done!"

Erika's cheer was the bell announcing the end of the lesson.

"Hoo... *Danke*, Tatsuya!"

Tatsuya lifted a hand to Leo's word of thanks and addressed Miyuki. She was coming this way with a smile. Her two classmates, Honoka Mitsui and Shizuku Kitayama, followed with their own smiles, though hesitant.

"Excellent work, both of you," she congratulated Erika and Leo, then asked, "Tatsuya, I've brought what you asked for... But is this enough?"

Tatsuya shook his head. "Well, there's not much time left anyway, so it's about the right amount. Thank you for coming, Miyuki. And Mitsui and Kitayama, as well. I apologize for making you help me out."

He had already gotten to the point where he'd seen them around and spoken to them on occasion, but the two surrounding Miyuki were still only acquaintances; they weren't yet *friends* to him. That was why he seemed a bit reserved when he spoke to them.

"No, not at all—this was nothing much!"

"We're okay. I'm actually pretty strong."

Honoka's answer came with unexpected strength, and Shizuku's with ambiguity as to whether she was serious or joking. He thanked both of them again, then took plastic bags from the three of them, including Miyuki.

"Here." He held them out to Erika and Leo.

"What?"

"Sandwiches...?"

Inside the bags were sandwiches and drinks they sold at the store.

"If we went to the cafeteria to eat, we wouldn't make it back in time for our afternoon classes," he said, taking a bento box from Miyuki.

"Aw, thanks! I was totally starving!"

"Tatsuya, you're the best!"

He gave a dry grin to his mercurial friends, then sat down in a nearby chair when Mizuki, too, addressed him in a reserved way. "...Is this all right? Aren't food and drink not allowed in the training rooms?"

"That's just for the area around the information terminals. School rules don't have much to say about eating and drinking in the classroom."

"Wait, is that true?"

"Yeah. Reading the school rules carefully would tell you that. I completely thought it wouldn't be allowed myself, so I was a little surprised," answered Tatsuya calmly, picking up his chopsticks. Mizuki was convinced and held out her hands.

"Huh... Well, in that case, don't mind if I do!" Leo unwrapped his sandwich and began to devour it.

"Please, you wouldn't have minded anyway," retorted Erika, biting into her sandwich in an oddly refined fashion.

At the lively table—well, they didn't have a table, so they brought over some chairs—Tatsuya and the rest of the party that had stayed behind began their late lunch.

Miyuki and the suppliers had brought just drinks for themselves and joined the circle.

"Did you three already eat?" asked Mizuki, probably in consideration.

"Yes. I was told by my brother to eat before him," answered Miyuki.

"Hmm, that's a little unexpected. I thought for sure you'd say something like *I could not possibly partake of my food before my brother!*" Erika's retort was spoken with more of a smirk than a grin.

They could tell from her face she wasn't serious. Those who heard her didn't reply seriously, either.

—Except for one person.

"Oh my, you really understand, Erika. Normally, you'd be right, of course, but I did so today at my brother's command. I cannot reject my brother's words with my own selfish hesitations."

"...Normally..."

"Yes."

"...'Of course,' huh...?"

"Yes, that's right, why?"

Erika's smirk was starting to cramp, and Miyuki replied to her with seriousness, tilting her head to the side.

As if to wipe away the suddenly much heavier air, Mizuki began to talk in an unnaturally high tone of voice. "Miyuki, your class started practice today, too, right? What were you all doing?"

Honoka and Shizuku exchanged glances.

Their expressions were tinged with awkward reserve.

Miyuki, though, contrary to her classmates' attitudes, didn't make a big deal out of it; she lifted her lips from her straw and answered immediately. "I don't think it was any different from what you all were doing, Mizuki. We were provided a dull-witted device and made to do boring practice that could never have any practical use outside a test environment."

Everyone aside from Tatsuya looked taken aback. Those were blistering remarks for one who portrayed herself as a proper lady.

"You seem like you're in a bad mood."

"Yes, and I am displeased. The exercise would have been more useful to practice alone," answered Miyuki, smiling, to her brother's almost-teasing words, speaking in a pouty—and yet still obvious to onlookers, a fawning—voice.

"Huh… Maybe all that tutoring wasn't such a good thing."

"I will admit that I am blessed. I apologize if I've offended you," said Miyuki, bowing seriously.

"No, no, you didn't offend me at all," replied Erika, waving a hand lightly.

"It's only natural they'd separate the students with potential. Even in our dojo, people without potential get left alone."

"Erika, your family runs a dojo?" asked Mizuki.

"It's a side job, but yeah, we do a little of the old style of *kenjutsu*."

"Oh, so that's why…" Mizuki nodded, convinced. She was probably thinking of when Erika smacked Morisaki's CAD out of his hands with her extending baton.

"Chiba… You think it's only natural?" That was Honoka, hesitantly getting a few words in.

"You can call me Erika. Actually—I command you to call me that!"

"What do you keep acting so high and mighty for?"

Leo's exasperated retort seemed to give Honoka just enough time to recompose herself. "Then you can call me Honoka, too, Erika."

"Okay, got it! It's natural, and maybe that's why Course 1 kids get instructors and Course 2 kids don't?"

"…Yes, that's right," said Honoka slowly, nodding.

"Then it's only natural, right?" said Erika, nodding without any reservation. "It's the obvious thing to do, so I don't see why you or Miyuki need to feel bad about it," she declared absently.

"…You really put things bluntly, eh?" asked Leo.

"Hmm? Leo, are you just mad about how things are?"

"No, I don't think there's any other option either, but…" His answer was stammered, unusually for him.

"I *see*! But I think it's only natural, not that there's no other option," she answered, crisply and smoothly.

"…May I ask why?" said Honoka.

Erika cocked her head to the side. After a short silence to let her get her thoughts in order, she scratched at a temple with a finger and said, "Hmm… I've just thought it was only natural this whole time, so it's a little hard to explain… Well, like, our dojo doesn't teach skills for at least half a year after students join."

"That right?" nodded Tatsuya, very interested.

"We only teach how to move your feet and practice swings at the beginning. And we only have to show them one time, and then watch as they do their practice swings over and over. Then, if they get to a point where they can really wield a katana, we start teaching them skills."

"…But then wouldn't there be students who would never get to that point no matter how long they tried?"

"Yeah, there are!" nodded Erika to Honoka's question. "And those kind of people—they want to ignore their own lack of effort. The thing is, if they don't get used to the motion of swinging a katana and moving their bodies, then they'll never grasp the skills we try to teach them."

"Oh…" grunted Mizuki.

Erika glanced at her, then continued. "And to do that, they need to swing a katana on their own. They learn how by watching. There's plenty of examples all around them. It wouldn't make any sense to wait for something to be taught to you. And thinking you'll be taught from the beginning is a naive way of thinking, too. The instructors and the masters are people currently in training themselves, you know? They have their own training to do. Guys who can't absorb what they're taught would be talking nonsense if they asked for someone to teach them."

Tatsuya watched quite interestedly as Erika, suddenly excited, went on and on with her strong declarations.

"...Thanks for the explanation, I guess, but both you *and* me were just getting Tatsuya to teach us, remember?"

"Ack! Ouch! It hurts when you say that." Leo's indication made her grimace, but her absent attitude didn't change. "I mean, that was, like, something we had to do to get out of the immediate problem we were having... But I think if the person you're teaching isn't at a suitable level for you to teach them, then it'll end up bad for both ends. Well, the worst thing is when the one teaching can't keep up with the one being taught."

She gave a quick, meaningful wink.

Tatsuya smirked in an ill-natured way. "Unfortunately, it looks like we got the worst result today. In the end, my record was over a hundred milliseconds slower than yours, Erika."

A thin bead of cold sweat ran down Erika's temple. "Oh, uh, I wasn't, I didn't mean that... C-come to think of it, you didn't reveal how the trick worked! Hey, why did my time go down so much just by putting my other hand on top?"

She forced the topic to change.

It was clear to everyone she was diverting the conversation, but it seemed like if they persisted too much, they'd be feeling the unpleasant effects of it much later, so Tatsuya obediently let the topic be changed.

"What? It's simple. You're used to a one-handed style for your CAD."

Tatsuya's "revelation" had only just begun, but the one who had asked for the explanation, Erika, went "Huh?" and interrupted.

Her expression was asking him how he knew that, but he thought it was something one would naturally notice at first glance. Both the action she'd shown when they were facing Morisaki and her CAD's form itself led him to easily guess the style she preferred with CADs. He ignored Erika's slightly exaggerated reaction and continued his "revelation." "So I thought that maybe you couldn't smoothly access the kind of classroom CAD where you put both hands on the panel."

"So by putting her hands on top of each other, you made it so she was only contacting it in one place…" Mizuki nodded in admiration. She wasn't the only one giving him that look, though.

"Using only one hand would have worked, too, but I figured you'd get more pumped up if you put your hands on top of each other. In other words, it was all in the attitude."

"…I get it. You played me like a fiddle, Tatsuya."

Erika gave an empty grin.

Her sudden exhaustion was very comic-like, and it caused everyone else to smile.

"Yeah, I kind of don't care anymore… Oh, right. Did you use the same CAD as this in Class A?"

"Yes," said Miyuki, nodding, not bothering to hide her aversion to it.

That piqued Erika's curiosity. "Hey, just curious, but could you try it out here so I can see what kind of time you get?"

"What? Me?" responded Miyuki, pointing at herself, her eyes growing wide.

Erika nodded unnaturally deeply.

Miyuki used her eyes to ask Tatsuya.

"Why not?" he nodded, giving a dry grin.

"If you say so, Tatsuya…" she responded hesitantly, indicating her understanding.

Mizuki, who was closest to the machine, set up the scale.

Miyuki placed her fingers on the panels as though she were going to play the piano.

Measurement began.

The excess psions flashed...

...and Mizuki's face froze.

Impatient with her friend not announcing the results, Erika read out the results.

"...Two hundred thirty-five milliseconds..."

"What...?"

"Crazy..."

The facial-muscle petrification infected the others as well.

"That's amazing, no matter how many times I hear it..."

"Miyuki's processing abilities are close to the limit of human reaction speed."

The students from A class sighed to themselves as well.

Her brother was the only one who wasn't surprised. The girl in question frowned, unsatisfied. "I suppose that's as good as it will get with an old educational one like this. Give it up, Miyuki," said Tatsuya.

"I simply cannot bear it... I cannot stand needing to take in an activation program like this, with so much surface noise and not a hint of polish or sophistication. I truly cannot display the full extent of my abilities without using a CAD that you have adjusted, Tatsuya."

"Don't say that. I'll negotiate with the president and the chairwoman on the school side of things to try and get the software switched out with something a little more usable."

Tatsuya softly stroked Miyuki's face, which was twisted in both sullenness and sweetness, like a small child.

Like always, despite the display, nobody went after them.

Not for the showing of her real abilities, and not for the words exchanged between the siblings.

Given the profound difference, it was absurd to even *think* about being jealous.

◇ ◇ ◇

Tatsuya lazily watched the students coming and going in the cafeteria after school. There was an air of awkwardness about, perhaps because it was used by many of the new freshmen. From what Mari had told him, the school cafeteria saw its highest utilization rate right after school started. As they got used to it, they would find hangouts in rooms, courtyards, and empty classrooms, and stop coming as much. *Well, they're not running the place for profit, so they probably don't care about having fewer guests.*

The coffee on his table had already grown cold. He'd been placed into the reverse situation as yesterday. The only part that was the same was that *he'd* been the one invited this time. Tatsuya was currently waiting for Sayaka to hear her answer for her "homework."

There was an annoying gaze watching him, following him around, but he didn't take any particular action from his end. He was confident that if he cared enough, he could find who was spying on him, no matter what tricks they used to hide him- or herself. However, the cafeteria was an open space, so even if he caught the culprit, he knew they'd just feign ignorance. Rather than fruitlessly reveal his own intentions, it would be wiser to wait quietly and pretend he didn't notice.

Fifteen minutes from the agreed-upon time, she finally showed up.

"I'm sorry! Were you waiting?"

"It's all right. I got your message."

He wasn't lying to make her feel better. His terminal had received a message to the effect that she'd be around ten minutes late. It had come five minutes before they were going to meet, though, so it didn't give him any time to change his plans. Tatsuya was patient, however—ten or twenty minutes barely even counted as waiting for him.

"I see, that's good… I wouldn't know what to do if you got mad and left." Sayaka heaved an exaggerated sigh of relief.

It seemed like she was in her "cute girl" mode again today. *She's*

been putting on this performance for a while. What does she think I'm into?
wondered Tatsuya.

"What's wrong?" She sounded confused.

It looked like his thoughts had shown in his movements. "It's nothing important. Sometimes you turn into a cute girl, and I was feeling the gap between that and when you're holding a sword."

"Oh, come on... Stop teasing me." With a hint of fluster, she turned her eyes away.

Was that an honest response, or was it an affected act, too? He couldn't tell. Unfortunately, his probing had fallen through.

"I'm sorry," he apologized with a smile. This was his own act. He didn't have much confidence in it, though.

"Geez... Shiba, deep down you're a womanizer, aren't you?"

"Well, I'm not a magician. Not yet, anyway."

He put his cooled coffee to his lips and slowly turned around. He wasn't trying to look away from Sayaka as much as he was glancing at the shadow peeking out from behind some decorative plants.

"Watanabe..." Sayaka noticed the shadow a moment later, too. Her voice was too soft, though, so it didn't reach the ears of the one she'd spoken the name of.

"'Sup, Tatsuya?"

Mari was the first one to speak. But that was clearly a challenge; if he hadn't clearly looked over there, she probably would have passed by with a look of indifference—if that wasn't the case, then she wouldn't have tried to keep out of sight.

"I'm not slacking off."

Mari gave a pained grin to Tatsuya's response. He actually meant "I'm not on duty today," but she found it difficult to decide if it was a joke or if he was acting rebelliously. "I didn't come to give you a warning as the chairwoman or anything. I just happened to be passing by."

But thanks to what he had said, Mari's appearance had stopped feeling unnatural. And Mari, who could get with things on the spot like that, was pretty impressive.

"Sorry, it seems like I interrupted something. I apologize, Mibu."

"No, you didn't..." Sayaka's voice in reply and her expression had stiffened up a little at Mari, maybe out of nervousness from being addressed by an upperclassman. Or maybe it was antipathy toward the disciplinary committee.

Tatsuya, for whatever reason, felt like neither of those was quite accurate.

His impression was strengthened by the powerful gaze she fired toward Mari's back as she left.

"About the other day..."

Once Mari had left the cafeteria, Sayaka broached the main topic herself. Tatsuya had been late in doing so, since he was thinking things like *I was the one who asked* and *I can't believe she'd come to check up on me...* and *Was she keeping an eye on something else?*

"At first, I thought just telling the school what we thought would be enough." Her arms twitched—maybe she'd clenched her fists under the table or something. "But I realized that wouldn't be enough, after all. I think we should demand reform in how the school treats us."

Right to the point was Tatsuya's impression. Was she serious, or was it a bluff to draw him in? If it was a bluff, it had the opposite effect. "When you say *reform*, what exactly would you like to be changed?"

"Well...everything about how we're treated."

"When you say *everything*, you mean classes, for example?"

"...Well, that, too."

"The main difference between Course 1 and Course 2 is the presence of an instructor. Given that, are you asking for more teachers from the school?"

That was impossible. The national school policy was a direct result of there not being enough adults who could use magic at an effective level in the first place. The two-course system was, in a way, a plan created in full knowledge of the drawbacks in order to secure a supply of magicians and magic engineers.

"I don't plan on going that far, but…" As expected, he received a stammered denial in reply.

"Then is it club activities? Aren't the kendo club and the *kenjutsu* club allotted the same amount of time to use the gymnasium?" As far as he'd looked into it yesterday, the days allotted to the kendo and *kenjutsu* clubs—surprisingly enough—were distributed equally.

"Or is it a budget issue? It's true that magic competition clubs are given bigger budgets compared to other clubs, but I believe budget distribution based on club achievement isn't unusual to see even in normal high schools."

"Well that's… That may be true, but… Aren't you unhappy with it, Shiba? You're superior to Course 1 students in every way aside from practical application—like magical theory, general subjects, physical fitness, and skill in actual combat. And yet just because you're bad at application, you get looked down on as a Weed. Isn't that frustrating for you?"

Her desperate, vehement argument made Tatsuya feel a little irritated. His dissatisfaction and resentment had nothing to do with how she felt. If she was the one who wanted to change things, then why wasn't she talking about herself? "Of course I'm not happy with it."

But he—

"Then…!"

"But there is nothing I really want to have the school change."

—spoke of his own feelings.

"Huh?"

"I never expected all that much from a school as an educational institution." It was no more than a piece of a fragment, but they were his true thoughts. "I don't need anything more than the ability to view private documents and materials you can only look at from places affiliated with the National Magic University, and to gain the right to graduate from Magic High School."

Sayaka's face froze up at his detached—even to himself—statement.

"And I certainly don't plan on blaming the school for the childish nature of my classmates for using hurtful slang prohibited by the school."

At first, those words appeared to be criticizing the mistaken elitism of the Blooms looking down at the Weeds, but in reality, he was blaming Sayaka's own weakness for trying to make her own dissatisfaction the fault of someone else.

"Unfortunately, it would seem we do not share a common position on this." With that, Tatsuya rose from his seat.

"Wait!"

He turned around to see Sayaka looking up at him with a pale, clinging gaze, still seated—maybe she couldn't get up. She wasn't glaring—it was a look of pure sincerity and desperation. "How...can you think so rationally about it? What on earth do you have to support you?"

"I would like to make a gravity-controlled thermonuclear fusion reactor a reality. Studying magic is no more than a means to that end."

Sayaka's face blanked out. She probably hadn't understood what she'd just been told.

The actualization of a gravity-controlled thermonuclear fusion reactor was one of the so-called Three Great Practical Problems of Weighting Magic, along with the realization of multipurpose flight magic and the realization of a pseudo-perpetual motion device by inertial infinitization. It was far too big a project for a Course 2 student to suggest as a future goal.

And Tatsuya hadn't said what he did because he wanted her to understand. Without bothering any more with Sayaka, he turned back around.

A week passed without incident.

His disciplinary committee patrols saw none of the ambush-like attacks from the recruitment week, and as Mizuki prophesied (?), everything was mostly peaceful. Finally, Tatsuya had gotten his hands on his quiet high school life—or so it seemed. It was, in hindsight, no more than a momentary tranquillity.

It was right after classes ended, just at the start of what could be called "after school."

Students who had club after this were going to their lockers to change or grab their things, and those who had brought in tablets and paper notebooks were grabbing their bags from the sides of their desks. Those who did neither were casually getting ready for the trek home, each in his or her own way. That was when it happened.

"Attention all students!"

A loud voice just short of howling burst from the speaker.

"What the hell was that?!"

"Would you calm down already? You're basically yelling yourself!"

"…I think you should calm down, too, Erika."

The many students still in the room were busy being confused.

"—Please excuse me. Attention all students!"

Once more, this time a little awkwardly, they heard the same line from the speaker.

"They must have messed up the volume control," muttered Tatsuya lowly.

Erika keenly picked up on his words and immediately went for the jab. "Uh, I don't think this is the time for witty jokes."

Mizuki found herself unable to actually say, "That goes for you, too, Erika" aloud.

"We are a coalition of the willing who aim to abolish discrimination at school."

"The willing…" muttered Tatsuya cynically after hearing the assertive voice of the male student from the speaker. Judging by what he'd heard last week in the cafeteria, this broadcast hijacking was for the treatment reform demands that Sayaka had talked about. He couldn't help but wonder, though, just how many examples in all of history there were of members who were part of political organizations voluntarily becoming a "coalition."

"We hereby declare our desire for negotiations on equal terms with the student council and the club committee."

"Hey, shouldn't you, like, go?" Erika expectantly asked Tatsuya, who was sitting and looking at the speaker. She probably hadn't heard his unfriendly murmur, though.

"I suppose so." He didn't say that her attitude was imprudent; what she'd said had been reasonable. "They've obviously misappropriated the broadcasting room. The disciplinary committee will—" At the exact moment he spoke, a message arrived on the portable terminal in his pocket rather than on the information terminal fixed on the desk. "Oops, speak of the devil. I should get going."

"Oh, okay. Be careful." Mizuki's voice trembled with unease as Tatsuya rose from his seat and turned away from them. Suddenly concerned, he turned around and scanned the classroom. Some of his classmates were sitting and some were standing, but not many looked like they were about to leave the classroom. There were few others who were bemused like Erika or curious like Leo. Most of his classmates looked anxious, unable to decide whether they should just get home.

"Oh, Tatsuya!"

"Miyuki, you got called here, too?"

"Yes, by the president. She told me to go to the broadcast room."

Part of the way there, he met up with Miyuki and they headed toward the broadcast room. They weren't moving very quickly, however.

"Could this be Blanche's doing?"

"We can't be sure of what group is behind this, but they would certainly do this kind of thing."

They were still talking about it as they arrived in front of the broadcasting room together. Mari, Katsuto, and Suzune were already there, as well as others from the disciplinary committee's and club committee's active units.

"You're late."

"Sorry."

He returned the superficial reprimand with a superficial apology and started coming to terms with the situation.

The broadcast had stopped, likely because they'd cut the electricity. They probably hadn't gone inside yet because the door was barricaded. The culprits who trapped themselves inside must have gotten hold of a master key somehow.

"This is clearly a criminal act, isn't it?" They let the ends justify the means—model activists.

Tatsuya had been talking entirely to himself, but Suzune didn't hear it that way. "That's right. We must respond carefully so that we don't set them off any more than this."

"I don't have much faith that being careful will cause them to listen to reason," put in Mari immediately. "We should devise a quick solution, even if it means getting a little rough."

Their difference in opinions appeared to put them at an impasse. It was an incredibly clumsy way of dealing with the emergency.

"What do you have in mind, Chairman Juumonji?"

Looks filled with surprise turned on Tatsuya at his question. Even Tatsuya had wondered if he'd stepped out of line as he'd asked it, but he figured it was better than staying in this deadlock. It must have meant that he was no adult, either. And this wasn't a situation in which they could ask an adult to intervene.

"I'm thinking we should respond to their demands for negotiation. We don't have many clues in the first place. Firmly arguing against them may allow us to eliminate future worries."

"Then you say we should wait here like this?"

"I am unsure what decision to make in that regard. We should not let unauthorized conduct be, but I don't believe this crime deserves a hasty resolution if it means destroying school property. I inquired as to whether or not the school could open the door using the security surveillance system, but I was denied a response."

That meant they couldn't force a resolution for the situation. Accordingly, Katsuto's stance was close to that of Suzune's. Then they couldn't do anything but wait like this.

Tatsuya gave a polite bow and stepped back, and Mari shot him with an unhappy stare. He hadn't been urged on by her thorny gaze, but he took his portable terminal out of his pocket and booted it into call mode.

They could only wait, but if they weren't going to do anything else, he wouldn't have stood up and asked the question.

The call tone rang five times, then connected. "Is this Mibu? It's Shiba."

A few more surprised looks were directed at him.

"...And where are you now?"

Even more sets of perplexed eyes stared hard at him.

"I see—the broadcasting room. That is...unfortunate."

A moment later he grimaced—possibly because a loud voice had shouted back at him before the volume controller could kick in. They couldn't do any more than speculate, though, given the canal-shaped receiver was almost completely soundproof.

"No, I am not making fun of you. Mibu, please, consider the situation a little more calmly... Yes, I'm sorry. Now then, what I called you for..."

Mari's, Suzune's, and a few others' ears perked up. They must have known they still wouldn't be able to hear the voice on the other end, but they didn't want to let a single word Tatsuya said slip by them.

"Chairman Juumonji has stated that he will accept negotiations. We still don't know the student council president's opinion—oh, the student council president thinks the same way." Suzune gestured and Tatsuya immediately corrected himself. "With that said, they'd like to meet with you to determine a time and place for the negotiations... Yes, right now. That way the school won't have to get involved... No,

I can guarantee your freedom, Mibu. We're not the police, so we can't throw you behind bars or anything... All right."

He took his ear from his calling unit and stowed the device along with the rest of his terminal, then turned back to Mari. "She said they'll come out right away."

"Was that Sayaka Mibu?"

"Yes. She gave me her private number so that we could meet, but it seems to have come in handy for another reason."

Behind him, Miyuki cast her eyes down a little. It wasn't so pronounced that it would seem unnatural, but he immediately knew she was doing it to hide her irritation behind her long hair.

"You're a quick worker, you are..."

"You misunderstand." Tatsuya didn't notice it, however, since his awareness had been partially on Mari's false accusation—for better or worse. At the very least, she had the good sense not to recklessly give him a sharp pinch in the back or anything. "Anyway, I think we should get ready."

Without looking behind him (in other words, at Miyuki), he suggested their next course of action to Mari, Suzune, and Katsuto.

"Get ready?" Mari looked at him, wondering what he was saying.

Tatsuya looked back at her, exasperated, wondering what *she* was saying. "We need to get ready to arrest them. They *stole a key*. They probably brought their CADs with them, and they might have other weapons, too."

"...I thought you just said something along the lines of guaranteeing their freedom."

"The only person I guaranteed freedom to was Mibu. Also, I didn't suggest anything that would imply I was negotiating on behalf of the disciplinary committee."

This time, not only Mari, but Suzune and Katsuto as well, were taken aback.

The only exception present chided him lightly. "You're a bad person, Tatsuya."

"It took you long enough to notice, Miyuki."

"Hee-hee, I suppose so." Her tone of voice, though, was tinged with amusement.

"However, Tatsuya, regarding how you saved Mibu's private number to your terminal—that is a different matter. You *will* tell me all about it later, won't you?" added Miyuki with a broad smile and an even more amused tone of voice.

"What's going on here?!"

Perhaps as they'd expected, and perhaps as was only natural, Sayaka pressed Tatsuya for an explanation.

Including her, there had been five people taking over the broadcasting room. As Tatsuya had thought, they possessed CADs, but didn't have any other firearms or bladed weapons with them. Tatsuya personally felt that showed a complete lack of resolve, but they didn't think they were doing anything wrong, so maybe it was a matter of course that their efforts had been unsatisfactory.

The four aside from Sayaka were arrested by members of the disciplinary committee, but they only confiscated Sayaka's CAD. Mari had given consideration to Tatsuya's reputation, and this was the result. Tatsuya himself felt he didn't necessarily need to keep any oral promises, though.

Sayaka's hands were reaching for his chest, and Tatsuya held her wrists in his. He had smoothly grabbed the hands trying to grab his collar, and he looked back at her indignation without expression.

"You tricked us!" She struggled to break her hands free, and Tatsuya simply let them go. She tried to complain further, but a voice addressed her from behind.

"Shiba has not tricked you."

The heavy, strong tones caused Sayaka to tremble briefly. "Chairman Juumonji…"

"We will hear your excuses. We will also accept your negotiations. But acquiescing to your demands and accepting the actions you've taken as proper are separate issues."

Sayaka's aggressiveness faded. She swallowed her anger at the power of Katsuto, the overseer of all extracurricular activities.

"That may be true, but could I get you to release them?"

But then, with those words, a petite person stepped between Tatsuya and Sayaka. She had her back turned to him, as if to shield him.

"Saegusa?" Katsuto said dubiously.

"But Mayumi…" Mari began to argue.

Mayumi cut her argument off before it could begin. "I think I know what you want to say, Mari. But Mibu can't meet with us to plan the negotiations by herself. And she's a student of this school; she can't run away."

"We would never run away!" Sayaka snapped reflexively at her.

Mayumi, however, didn't directly respond to her words. "I've just returned from consulting with the head life coach. They will apparently leave the matter of the stolen key and the use of the broadcasting facility without permission to the student council."

Her explanation was nonchalant, describing both her lateness and the position they were currently placed in. Still, Sayaka and the others didn't show fear. Regardless of the right or wrong of the situation, Tatsuya felt that their nerves of steel were praiseworthy.

"Mibu, I would like for you all to meet with the student council regarding the negotiations; could you come along with me?"

"…Yes, we will."

"Juumonji, I will see you later, okay?"

"Understood."

"I'm sorry, Mari. I hesitated to do this because it seemed like I'd be stealing your glory."

"I may feel like that just a little bit, but practically speaking, there's no advantage to getting any glory. Don't worry about it."

"You're right. All right. Tatsuya, Miyuki, you two may feel free to leave for the day."

There was a very short period of time where they were surprised, and Miyuki was the first one to recover from the situation. "...Thank you, President. We will take our leave." She gave a polite bow. Tatsuya silently followed suit, then they left.

[9]

The next day, Tatsuya and Miyuki left the house earlier than usual.

Not to get to school early, but to get to the station early.

Fortunately, they didn't have to wait very long.

"Good morning, President."

Mayumi was small in stature even for a girl, but she wasn't the sort who would get lost in a crowd. Her silhouette gave off a much stronger sense of presence than others, allowing Tatsuya to pick her out immediately.

"Tatsuya? Miyuki, too. What's the matter?"

Their ambush seemed to come as a surprise to Mayumi—well, of course it did. She had no leeway to put together her usual jovial attitude, and instead gave an unsophisticated, unexceptional response to them.

Surprising her wasn't their goal this morning, though. Tatsuya didn't bother with any needless fooling around and got to the point right away. "I was wondering about yesterday. Would you tell me how your discussion with Mibu and the others after that ended up?"

At Tatsuya's demand, Mayumi's eyes widened a bit. "How surprising." Not only did it come out in her expression, it also came out in her words. "Tatsuya, you don't seem like the type of person to pry into the affairs of others."

"I wouldn't if it were unrelated, but that's not the case."

"I see." Upon hearing his answer, though, she nodded as though convinced. Tatsuya was already related in no small way to the activities of their "willing coalition." Even if he'd wanted to treat it as someone else's problem, they weren't going to let him off the hook. Mayumi agreed, feeling that he was entitled to hear what would happen now—and even if she hadn't, she was going to announce it to everyone first thing in the morning anyway. "They demand equal treatment of Course 1 and Course 2 students. But they don't seem to have given much thought to anything concrete they want to do. It actually felt more like they wanted the student council to work out the specifics. So it turned into a rather heated dispute. We had originally wanted to talk about negotiations afterward yesterday, so we ended up deciding on a public debate in the lecture hall after school tomorrow."

"Things escalated quickly…" The way in which Tatsuya was surprised could actually be called reserved. The impression coming from him was more one of "finally" than anything else, so he wasn't very surprised. He considered dragging them into a fair fight would lead to the quickest results and fastest resolution in the first place, even if it left a bad taste in some people's mouths. But his reaction was probably pretty in the minority. As a case in point, the development had not been something Miyuki had expected—her eyes were wide and she was unable to speak.

"I can understand the tactic of not giving those engaging in guerrilla warfare any time to spare, but that means we don't have time to think of a plan, either. Who from the student council will be participating in this debate?"

Tatsuya's question was answered with a smile that said *well done* from Mayumi. She pointed at her face.

"…You, by yourself, President?"

His tone was half-believing but half-dubious. And Miyuki was completely at a loss for words.

"I'll have Hanzou come up on stage with me, but I'll be the only one talking. Because, as you said, there's not enough time for a briefing. And by myself, there's no threat of us bumping heads against each other for slight discrepancies in viewpoints. I'd be afraid of emotions being brought in to manipulate impressions, in that case."

"So with a logical argument you cannot lose?" asked Tatsuya. Mayumi gave him a confident nod.

"And also," she continued lightly, her voice imbued with a hint of anticipation, "if they do happen to possess concrete evidence enough to defeat me, then all we have to do is incorporate that into managing the school."

It almost sounded to him like she was hoping she'd be out-argued.

Just after the announcement that the unprecedented debate would be held tomorrow, the coalition (as the "coalition of the willing who aim to abolish discrimination at school" came to be called) immediately energized its activities.

Though in an unrefined way, they tried to increase their supporters as well—coalition members recruiting sympathizers began to be seen in every nook and cranny of the school before classes, during breaks, and after school.

They all wore white wristbands with blue and red edges. Tatsuya wondered if they decided it wasn't worth hiding anymore or if they just didn't know what the symbol meant—he thought it was the former. He still couldn't agree with the thinking that ignorance was an excuse, though. He believed blame to be attached to actions rather than an internal thing.

However, it didn't necessarily make him want to hamper the coalition's actions. It was only natural they'd want to get their hands on many sympathizers and "have a discussion" with them. He had no intention of interfering with people unrelated to him who were deluding emotionally immature high school students with emotional words and dragging them down into a bottomless swamp. (Though that was a terrible thought in a number of ways.)

On the other hand, if it *was* someone he was related to—though as a student of First High, nothing that happened in the school was *really* unrelated—he was not about to allow these deceptive temptations.

"Mizuki."

After school, on the day before the debate, he spotted a confused freshman being spoken to by what was likely a senior wearing the wristband in question on his right hand. Mizuki was clutching some sort of paintings to her chest, so she was probably in the middle of delivering things for her club. The fact they were using non-digital materials in this day and age probably meant there were more than a few people in the school art club who preferred it that way, but that didn't matter right now.

"Oh, Tatsuya!"

She saw him and gave a relieved expression. Judging by her look, she'd been wrapped up with this for a fair amount of time.

First, Tatsuya scanned the upperclassman from his head down. He was tall, and though at first glance he would seem scrawny, he actually had a body trained in martial arts.

He'd seen that figure before.

It was none other than the male student who had attacked him with magic and fled during the absolute nonsense that was the club recruitment week.

"I am Shiba, from the disciplinary committee. If you keep her for too long, you may be seen as a nuisance, so please step back."

He suddenly addressed the upperclassman without stopping to glance at Mizuki's expression. Still, though, he didn't try and interrogate him about the incident that happened during the new student recruitment week. He would never have admitted to anything even if Tatsuya did ask, and if he turned around and said they were false accusations, it would have the opposite effect. Tatsuya slid between Mizuki and the upperclassman with an air of nonchalance and faced him directly.

There was no emblem on his left breast.

On his face were small, square glasses. They didn't look fake.

"All right. I'll leave for now. Miss Shibata, I am free at any time, so if you change your mind, give me a call."

The upperclassman was acting supremely gentlemanly (though more the Italian kind than the British kind) and pulled back. Once his departing figure disappeared from the hallway into the stairwell, he asked Mizuki about everything.

"He's the captain of the kendo club. He said his name was Kinoe Tsukasa... He has pushion radiation sensitivity, too. He wanted to know if I would be part of a circle he made with other students with sensitivities."

Tatsuya didn't expect Mizuki to come out and reveal the issue with her "eyes" herself. However, he was already convinced she had pushion radiation sensitivity, so he wasn't all that surprised.

"And what did he say? That you should share your burdens?"

"No, he said that his symptoms had improved a lot since entering the circle, so maybe it would help me, too..."

"Oh my." *Pretty sketchy*, he didn't say.

He didn't need to say it to understand Mizuki felt the same.

For the obstructions caused by magic-related senses being too sharp, controlling those sensing abilities was the one and only way to combat it. And in order to come to be able to control that ability, proper training was the fastest route.

Even without personal care from an instructor, the school's program was the closest to "proper training" you could get, so it was rather hard to think that a small circle of students could provide an even more effective regimen. It would be one thing if the circle had an instructor to guide them, but the whole reason behind the Courses 1 and 2 split in the first place was the hopeless lack of teaching faculty.

"I told him a few times I was too busy with classes..."

"Right. It's better to not be greedy and go along one step at a time, right?"

Mizuki nodded in agreement with his commonplace advice and headed for her club room.

Tatsuya started walking in the other direction and thought. It was probably coincidence that he'd come across her being accosted. But everything other than that couldn't have been a coincidence. The whole "circle" business was no more than a front, or perhaps bait; doubtless the kid's real plan was to lure her into their group. Judging by how the coalition had taken the practical measure of attacking him before going active, that senior was the real thing. At the very least, he wasn't someone who'd been lured in, but someone who did the fishing.

The captain of the kendo club, Kinoe Tsukasa …

I need to try looking into this senior in depth, he thought, making up his mind.

After dinner, during the time he would have usually been washing off the sweat and dirt from the day, Tatsuya was speeding along on an electric bicycle he'd just bought.

His destination was the Yakumo temple.

He didn't go there on foot because other than early morning and the middle of the night, there would always be the eyes of train passengers and passersby. The use of magic without proper reason was an act that carried a criminal punishment. Even a minor wouldn't escape substantial punishment.

As for the criminal act of riding a motorcycle—it was not one at all. Traffic laws as of 2095 AD said that you could get a motorcycle license after graduating middle school. It wasn't age-based; instead, you fulfilled the requirement by completing your compulsory education.

Around his waist were wrapped arms that were slender, yet not the slightest bit bony. Two bulges from his sister pressed up against his back. Certainly in the throes of puberty, no doubt, but definitely something—yet not paltry, either. For a girl who had just turned fifteen (Mizuki was born in March), there was no doubt that they were at least more than average.

That didn't mean Tatsuya's heart was trying to pound its way out of his chest, though. She was his little sister by blood, so of course (?) not.

And the trip was only about ten minutes long. With nothing immoral occurring either mentally or physically, the two of them arrived at the Yakumo temple.

The usual rough greeting at the gate didn't happen. This visit wasn't for training—they'd made an appointment by phone beforehand. Of course, there wouldn't be any polite greeting either, so they headed through the intimately familiar temple grounds for the priests' living quarters.

The Yakumo priest living quarters were based heavily on one-story residential building designs from the early twentieth century. They might have actually been constructed during that era; neither Tatsuya nor Miyuki had ever found out.

There was no light at all outside. And not because it was just old—it seemed intentional.

Not only were there no outdoor lights, but there was no light coming from the building, either. The night sky was cloudy, too, so no moonlight or starlight was shining, and the high walls blocked the city lights, making the temple grounds essentially pitch black.

It still wasn't so late they'd definitely be asleep, but maybe the priests went to bed as early as they awoke. He'd never heard of ninja maintaining an "early to bed, early to rise" attitude, and he couldn't imagine it, either. And besides, they'd promised they'd visit, so it was impossible that nobody was awake.

Miyuki softly extended a hand to Tatsuya's arm. The force of her grip on his sleeve wasn't very strong, nor was her hand shaking. Still, Miyuki didn't have the kind of night eyes Tatsuya did, so it wasn't hard to imagine she was feeling some instinctive anxiety at the darkness. —Well, even with one arm blocked off, he could just use his own inherent magic if it came to that, so he let his sister do as she pleased.

The temple grounds weren't cramped, but they weren't particularly wide, either. Before long, they arrived at the entrance to the living quarters. There was no video intercom, of course, but there wasn't even a doorbell—*that* was definitely intentional—so Tatsuya went to open the sliding door and announce their arrival. But as his hand touched the handle on the door...

"Over here, Tatsuya."

...he heard a voice calling him from the veranda, where he'd not sensed any presence before.

He felt a twitch on his arm through his grasped sleeve. Tatsuya, mildly exasperated, didn't feel like giving a dry grin. He was thinking to himself how childish it was for someone his age to be having fun scaring people by suddenly calling to them from the dark.

Of course, if Miyuki hadn't been the one to get surprised, Tatsuya probably wouldn't have felt anything. In that sense, his little scheme had been partially successful—if this was really a *scheme*, anyway.

Personally, he would have liked to do an about-face and leave, but he'd come here tonight for a reason. He swallowed back that bitter feeling and went around to the veranda toward where the voice came from.

The man would have looked a little like a priest if he'd been sitting cross-legged in meditation there, but he also thought this was more like Yakumo. Tatsuya had known him for two and a half years, but he was still an elusive one.

"Good evening, Master. Were you resting?"

"Hey, good evening, Tatsuya. And you, Miyuki. And no, not at all. Not even I would fall asleep after making a promise."

Yakumo brushed off Tatsuya's sarcastic remark so smoothly that it was Tatsuya who found it surprising, since he'd assumed he would be in and out of sight, slippery as an eel.

"Sensei, please excuse the late-night visit. If I may ask... If you were not resting, then why have you put out all the lights?"

"Hmm? Oh, it's custom. We don't turn on the lights when we don't need them. We're *shinobi*, after all."

Tatsuya had misunderstood that as mischief-making. He reflected a little on his mistake, telling himself that it was bad to let his own biases creep into his situational judgment, even if it normally happened differently.

Of course, he didn't breathe a word of that while Yakumo was watching.

The man didn't seem to notice anyway that Tatsuya had called his character into doubt. He looked up at the two of them, narrowed his eyes, then quietly spoke almost in a monotone. "Still, that prana you siblings have sure is something. It's even more splendid when you look at it without any lights around."

"Our prana?" asked Miyuki, tilting her head.

"It may be easier for you if I called it pushion emissions," answered Yakumo with an unusually serious expression. Narrowing his already narrow eyes wasn't a jealous expression at all, either—he was staring hard at "something" that was difficult to see. "Miyuki's prana glitters and shines, knowing no bounds, and there isn't a single unnecessary drop of Tatsuya's outside him. And connecting you—"

"Master," said Tatsuya suddenly, interrupting him.

Yakumo's narrowed eyes returned to their former state, and he gave a somewhat mischievous look. "Whoops, sorry, not allowed to go there, right?"

"No, I'm the one who should apologize for my rudeness." Tatsuya gave a slight bow, signaling the end of this discussion.

Of course, Yakumo understood it. "So what have you come for today?"

"Actually, there was something I wanted you to use your strength to look into," prefaced Tatsuya in answer to his question. He then explained Kinoe Tsukasa. "It's fairly certain this senior is a member of Égalité, but I think he also has a direct and strong link to Blanche. Would you happen to know through Kinoe Tsukasa what on earth Blanche might be planning?"

"Égalité and Blanche, eh... That's well within my means to investigate, of course." Yakumo nodded easily to Tatsuya's request phrased as a question. His words, too, could either be boastful or a rash promise, and it sounded natural for him to speak that way.

And Tatsuya knew that in reality, the man could do something so trivial as probing into terrorist organizations active domestically before breakfast.

"I am a man of the cloth, however. I don't get involved with the affairs of the common people. And if you've gotten that far already, wouldn't it be easier to ask Kazama? He has that young lady Fujibayashi with him, right?"

Tatsuya hesitated for a moment, then bitterly began, "...I'd rather not rely on the major—"

"Your aunt wouldn't sympathize?" interrupted Yakumo, not allowing Tatsuya to finish his sentence. "With the circumstances, I suppose you'd need to come here."

Tatsuya silently bowed his head. Not out of gratitude for his decision to listen to his request, but out of apology for his consideration.

Yakumo lightly waved a hand in front of him, suggesting apologies were unneeded, then gestured for Tatsuya and Miyuki to take a seat on the veranda.

Tatsuya sat next to Yakumo, and Miyuki, quite a bit more reserved than her brother, sat next to him; then Yakumo spoke.

"Kinoe Tsukasa...formerly known as Kinoe Kamono," he began without any preface. "Neither parent had any manifestation of magical factors. In other words, he's part of a 'normal' family, but it's a branch family of the Kamo. Although it is a branch, their blood relation is fairly thin, so there really isn't a problem with calling it a normal family. Kinoe's 'eyes,' though, were probably a kind of reversion."

Tatsuya's eyes widened—Yakumo was speaking as though he'd predicted his exact request—but he wasn't as surprised as his sister.

You couldn't keep up with Yakumo if you took the time to be surprised at everything the man said.

But he did still want to say this: "Master, have you ever heard of privacy?"

"Sure, I looked it up in a dictionary once."

Tatsuya's criticism had essentially ignored the fact that he was the one who was requesting an invasion of someone's privacy in the first place, and Yakumo played dumb without even a hint of guilt.

Both of the men decided not to look at Miyuki, who was holding a hand to her temple.

"Anyway, how did you know I would be asking you to look into Kinoe Tsukasa?"

The fact that Tatsuya changed the topic so abruptly showed how he wasn't able to *completely* ignore Miyuki's attitude.

Without objecting to the shift, Yakumo followed suit and put it behind them. "It didn't have anything to do with your request—I just know about him."

"...For what reason, may I ask?"

"Well, I'm a priest. At the same time—or rather, above that—I'm a *shinobi*. Fish cannot live without water, and *shinobi* cannot without a constant influx of information. I make a point of looking over people who have a history that might make them cause a problem in the right place at the right time."

Tatsuya narrowed his eyes just slightly. "Does that include us?"

Without raising his voice too much, Yakumo laughed, amused. "I tried to, but I didn't know what I was getting into. Information about the two of you has been perfectly manipulated. I suppose I should have seen that coming."

A somehow dubious air floated between the two of them. Miyuki hastily spoke, as though trying to get rid of that dark cloud. "Sensei, how are Tsukasa and Blanche related?"

Tatsuya's and Yakumo's faces softened at the same time at the atmosphere of Miyuki trying her best. They hadn't wanted to go at it for real anyway—they were glaring at each other jokingly. The feigned tension disappeared immediately.

His expression loosened, Yakumo answered Miyuki's question in a tone that suggested he was making small talk. "When Kinoe's mother remarried, her new husband brought his son, Kinoe's older stepbrother. He's the leader of Blanche's Japan branch. Not only as the outward-facing representative—he handles everything behinds the scenes, too. A real leader." In contrast to his lax expression, his answer was anything but peaceful. "Kinoe likely enrolled at First High due to the will of that stepbrother of his. They were probably aiming for something like what's going on now, but…I don't know exactly what it is they're planning. No doubt it's something wicked, though."

"I see…" Tatsuya slowly nodded to Yakumo's words, thinking about something.

"Sorry for not being able to give you the most important bit."

"No, you were a great help."

He wasn't just being diplomatic. He didn't think the man would be able to answer right away in the first place, and just the fact that Kinoe had been changed from "someone we *might* need to watch" to "someone we *need* to watch" meant a whole lot. He mentally jotted down a timetable—tomorrow, as early as he could before the debate, he'd casually recommend that Mari keep an eye on Kinoe Tsukasa.

Once that was settled, he realized there was one more thing he needed to ask. "By the way, Master. How strong are the abilities of Kinoe Tsukasa's 'eyes'?"

Yakumo put a hand to his chin at the question. It didn't seem like he was trying to put on airs; it looked like he was seriously thinking about it. "Let's see… Strong enough for me to see the pranic waves they emit, at least. He shouldn't have the power to read the prana hidden within you. At the very least, he doesn't have the kind of power to see prana that your classmate does, Tatsuya."

The last phrase Yakumo said caused Tatsuya to frown. "You've already investigated Mizuki, even?"

At that, Yakumo gave the most teasing, malicious smile he'd given all night. "You're interested, too, aren't you?"

Tatsuya barely fought back the urge to swear under his breath. It was obvious the man had seen right through him anyway, but letting it show in his attitude would be altogether galling.

"Interest" wasn't referring to the kind a boy would have in a girl of the same age. It was nothing so sexual as that. If he were to put it simply, Tatsuya was on guard against Mizuki. At her strange ability that could reveal the prana hidden inside him, just as Yakumo had suggested.

"I'll skip right to my conclusion and say that I don't think you need to be cautious around her." Tatsuya gritted his teeth, and that seemed to satisfy Yakumo. The man wasn't smiling anymore. His easygoing tone of voice and careless attitude were the same, but it wasn't the face of someone who would amuse himself with jokes or wordplay. "Even if she could see your prana, she wouldn't be able to understand it. If she were as well-versed in magic as you, she would know not to brandish her eyes recklessly."

The words had been intended to set his mind at ease, but Tatsuya found himself feeling doubtful. It was clear Yakumo hadn't meant to do that, but he felt like he'd been once again presented with the fact that he was a nonstandard article, something separate from the stereotypical magician.

[10]

And so the day of the public debate came. Half of all the students in the school gathered in the lecture hall.

"There's more here than I thought."

"More than anyone predicted, I think."

"To think our school has so many students with free time... Perhaps we need to propose a strengthening of the school's curriculum."

"That joke wasn't funny, Ichihara..."

In order, those were Miyuki's, Tatsuya's, Suzune's, and Mari's words. They were watching the scene from the stage wing. Mayumi stood a little bit away, waiting with Hattori. In the other wing were four seniors from the coalition, also waiting, under the watchful eyes of a disciplinary committee member. Sayaka was not among them.

"I wonder if they have others waiting somewhere else to use actual force..." muttered Mari, as if to herself. Only "as if"—it was clear she wasn't talking to herself.

"Agreed," muttered Tatsuya, understanding this fact. He was thinking the same thing.

He gave a quick look over the venue. The Course 1 students and Course 2 students were split about fifty-fifty. Leaving Suzune's joke aside, they hadn't thought so many students—not only Course 2, but Course 1 as well—were interested in this problem. Among them they identified about ten students as coalition members. And even among *them*, the members who had occupied the broadcasting room were nowhere to be seen.

"I don't know what they plan on doing…but we can't make the first move anyway."

That, too, was better left unsaid. The other side always had the initiative—all this side could do was wait for them to act.

"Nonaggressive security sounds good in theory, but…"

"Chairwoman Watanabe, please don't assume they will use force… It's beginning."

Mari had been about to argue against something—or rather, gripe about it—but she directed her gaze to the stage at Suzune's statement.

The debate, in the form of a panel discussion, naturally began like this:

"Student Council President, we have a question regarding budget distribution among clubs this autumn. According to the data we've gathered, competitive magic clubs with high ratios of Course 1 students are clearly given more of the budget than non-competitive magic clubs with high ratios of Course 2 students. This is evidence that preferential treatment of Course 1 students is not only prevalent in classes, but even in extracurricular activities, is it not?! President, if you really have equal treatment between Course 1 and Course 2 students in mind, then this unfair budget needs to be corrected immediately."

"Per-club budget distribution is decided upon by a council made up of every club president and based on budget ideas that take membership numbers and actual achievements into account. The reason it looks like competitive magic clubs are receiving more handsome budgets is largely a reflection of their intramural competition achievements. In addition, even nonmagic competitive clubs that have reached national levels of excellence like the legball team are given a budget just as high as competitive magic clubs. I believe this graph speaks for itself. The conclusion that Course 1 students are given preferential treatment when it comes to budget distribution is a mistaken one."

In this way, the flow reached a point where Mayumi, as representative of the student council, argued against the coalition's questions and demands.

Still, it wasn't as though the coalition had any concrete demands anyway. They only brought up budget distribution and said it should be done equally—they didn't have any demands as to which clubs, how much, or what portion of the budget should be added to theirs.

In the first place, it looked to Tatsuya like they'd been lured into this and dragged out here.

"Course 2 students are discriminated against in every way possible by Course 1 students. Aren't you just trying to deflect everyone from that fact?!"

"You stated *in every way possible*, but what, in particular, might you be referring to? As I've already explained, usage of our facilities and distribution of supplies is conducted on an equal basis from Class A all the way to Class H."

And their slogan, which would have been effective in the context of an agitated audience, was no more than empty idealism on stage. With Mayumi making her arguments using concrete examples and numbers that left no room for interpretation, their unsubstantial slogan stood no chance.

Before long, the debate had begun to turn into a speech for Mayumi instead.

"...I will not deny that there are those among the students who have the prejudice that the coalition has pointed out. However, this is a result of fixated senses of superiority and inferiority. It's created from the defensive instinct the privileged have—that their privilege will be encroached upon. It is wholly different from institutional discrimination.

"The terms *Bloom* and *Weed* are forbidden from use by the school, the student council, and the disciplinary officers, but unfortunately, many students use them anyway.

"However, the problem is *not only* that Course 1 students call themselves Blooms and decide to condescendingly call Course 2 students Weeds. Even Course 2 students scorn themselves as Weeds and accept it in resignation. It is a very sad tendency, and it exists."

A few people hooted, but nobody made an open argument.

The coalition had run out of arguments against Mayumi, who was concealing a coquettish, devilish smile, delivering an impassioned speech with a dignified expression and an imposing attitude.

"This wall in our minds is the real problem. Course 1 and Course 2 exist, clear as day, as part of the school system. However, this is due to there being a national shortage of teachers, which is not something that will be solved very soon. Either they give insufficient education to all, or give sufficient education to some. There is certainly a discrimination inherent in that.

"And there is nothing we can do about it. It's a regulation we need to accept as students of this school if we are to study here. But other than that point, there is no systematic discrimination. This may come as a surprise to some of you, but the curriculum for Course 1 and Course 2 students is exactly the same. There may be differences in how fast they progress, but it uses the same lectures and practices."

That was a surprise to both Tatsuya and Mayumi. He couldn't help but mutter "Huh..." under his breath, and she silently agreed with that sentiment. Suzune's mouth broke into a smile at seeing them.

"Even for extracurricular activities, the club committee and the student council assign facility usage as equally as we can. I won't deny that we do give preferential treatment to clubs with more members over those with less. However, that is a decision made because we can't ignore either individual opportunity or club-based opportunity. We do not and will not systematically prioritize magic-based extracurricular activities.

"Earlier, a member of the coalition mentioned that magic-based clubs were being given a heftier portion of the budget. He was correct in his conclusion, but I have already showed with a graph that the distribution is a result of their actual achievements being considered.

"Every issue aside from the teaching one can be explained through something other than the division between Course 1 and Course 2. I believe you now understand that there are rational, logical grounds for them. It is the wall in our minds that is the problem—our willingness to blame it on the Course 1/Course 2 division despite understanding there is another cause, which then distances Course 1 and Course 2 students from each other."

A few people hooted again. This time, though, some of the hoots were in agreement. The coalition supporters were jeering, but the voices coming from the cluster of Course 2 students present telling the coalition to shut up clearly displayed a shift in the way things were going.

"As the student council president, I am not satisfied with the current state of affairs. This mental wall can even incite hostility in school sometimes, so I've begun to want to solve this problem somehow. However, the solution must not be something that creates a new kind of prejudice. Even if Course 2 students were being discriminated against, reverse discrimination against Course 1 students is no solution. That cannot be permitted even as a temporary solution.

"Both Course 1 and Course 2 students belong to this school, and these are the only three years any of us will have as students here."

Applause broke out. There weren't enough people clapping to describe it as the entire audience applauding, but it was certainly not sparse. Among those clapping their hands, there was no division between Blooms and Weeds.

The wave of applause receded and silence came over the room. Both Course 1 and Course 2 students, both those who had clapped and those who had not, were staring fixedly at Mayumi up at the podium, eagerly awaiting her next words with bated breath.

The coalition panelists, on the same stage as her, glared at her, frustrated.

"I believe the only two things permitted to us are to remove the systematic discrimination and to not engage in reverse discrimination. This is an excellent opportunity, so I'd like it if you could all listen to my hopes.

"In all honesty, there is one last piece of the system that discriminates between Course 1 and Course 2 students in the student council—and that is the restriction on naming officers to non–student council groups. In the current system, all officer positions besides those in the student council must be nominated from Course 1 students. This rule is only part of the general assembly of the student council when a new student council president is elected, and we can change it. I plan to abolish this regulation during the assembly when I leave office. It will be my final job as student council president."

There was a stir. The students forgot to even hoot and jeer, and began whispering amongst themselves—to their fronts and backs, to their lefts and rights. Mayumi waited silently until the commotion died down naturally. "I've only been in this position for about half a year, so this commitment may sound premature. But we can't force people to change their minds, and we must not try. That's why I plan on tackling these reforms as much as I can using other means."

The entire lecture hall exploded into applause.

There was no shortage of cheers resembling those a fan club might give an idol, but it was clear that both Course 1 and Course 2 students supported not what the coalition had expressed, but what Mayumi had stated.

Mayumi was preaching about the upheaval of mental discrimination.

The actions of the coalition had certainly been the opportunity that allowed them to start on a path toward getting rid of discrimination. However, it was exactly the opposite of the kind of change they wanted. Reformist groups, even after accomplishing their goal, would gradually become unsatisfied with just that.

III

They were too caught up in achieving their goals using the methods they had imagined. The result was that this was unsatisfactory not so much to the coalition members but to those backing them.

—And besides, the masterminds who had incited Sayaka behind the scenes weren't planning to end things here, anyway.

Suddenly, an explosion rattled the windows of the lecture hall, and the students, letting themselves be engrossed in one action—their applause—awoke from their collective reverie.

The deployed disciplinary officers acted immediately.

With the kind of unified movements that seemed unbelievable since they hadn't gone through any kind of training, they restrained each marked coalition member.

A window shattered and a spindle-shaped object came flying in.

As the grenade hit the floor, it began spewing white smoke, but the smoke didn't scatter—instead, the grenade and the smoke all vanished back out the window, as if it were a videodisc being played backward.

Tatsuya looked over, praise in his eyes, and Hattori looked away from him, irritated. Mayumi couldn't help but giggle when she saw them.

Mari was facing the exit, her arm extended. Several intruders wearing gas masks all fell over as though they'd tripped on a stair and stopped moving.

The predicted assault had come with unexpected, extreme methods like explosives and chemical weapons, but as planned, it was quickly being put down. The panic in the room seemed like it would settle before being triggered.

"I'm going to check on the practicum building."

"I'll go with you, Tatsuya!"

"Be careful!" shouted Mari after the siblings as they headed for the area they'd heard the first explosion coming from.

Because magic high schools taught practical applications of magic, magicians were permanently stationed there as teachers. And with First High, seen as the highest magic high school, the teachers were all first-rate magicians as well. The school had the power to independently force out a small military group from a lesser nation. Of course, they might have accounted for the possibility of outside attackers, but they hadn't *predicted* that it would happen. In a place where nobody felt there would be an impending crisis, there was no real sense of caution.

The practicum building had easily surrendered control to the invading attackers belonging to the external faction. Its walls were scorched and its windows were in shards. The explosion Tatsuya had heard must have been a miniaturized explosive incendiary. The flames from it were still burning along one wall, and there were two teachers working on putting it out.

"The hell's going on here?" demanded Leo, who was engaged in a fierce, prolonged battle to guard those teachers when he got a glimpse of Tatsuya.

Miyuki's hands gracefully danced. With one hand she manipulated her portable terminal CAD. The psionic information bodies expanded, constructed, and were executed in the blink of an eye. The sparkling of magic, which only magic users—magicians and magic engineers—could see with the naked eye.

Three men surrounding Leo flew away all at once. They were dressed like electricians, and were clearly neither students nor faculty. They flew back with such force it looked like they'd stepped on a land mine, but Leo, in the middle of it all, wasn't affected at all. That pinpoint targeting was the biggest strong point of magic.

"Terrorists have infiltrated the school!" explained Tatsuya, very simply and cutting out the details, as Miyuki was talking to the teachers about something.

"Sounds pretty dangerous!" That was all it took to convince

Leo—Tatsuya knew he was the understanding sort from that over-time practice.

What was important right now was that there were enemies who needed to be eliminated.

"Leo, your *broom*! …Oh, reinforcements are here?"

Then, from the other direction where the office was, came Erika. She slowed her pace upon seeing Tatsuya and Miyuki there.

"Don't worry! You made it in time."

"Why would I worry? You wouldn't die even if they killed you!"

"What was that?! …Actually, there's no time to fool around. Just give me my CAD already—hey, don't throw it!"

CADs were delicate instruments, but they were also built with the premise of usage in tough environments in mind. They wouldn't break just from falling on a soft-coat path. Erika knew that, which is why she threw it to him, so she naturally ignored Leo's protest… though she probably would have ignored it even if it *could* have broken.

"Is this yours, Tatsuya? Or Miyuki's?" asked Erika simply, gazing at the moaning invaders crawling along the ground without even a hint of sympathy.

"Miyuki's. I'm not efficient enough for one of these."

"It's mine. I cannot bother my brother with dealing with these lowlifes."

Tatsuya's answer and Miyuki's, having come up beside him, were spoken at the same time.

"Right, right, what beautiful sibling love… So these guys, I can wipe 'em out, no questions asked, right?"

"No need for mercy as long as they're not students," Tatsuya answered, completely and thoroughly ignoring her wisecrack, glancing subtly away from her.

Erika grinned happily. "Hee-hee—and here I thought high school would be way more boring!"

"Whoa, scary. You sure are warlike, you know."

"You be quiet."

Erika had brought her right hand halfway up, but even she seemed to be cautious of hitting him with her specially-made baton.

"By the way, what were you two doing in the practicum building at a time like this?"

If they didn't have detention or make-up classes, the practicum building wasn't somewhere students had anything to do after school. He hadn't meant to ask it in a teasing, vengeful way—it was a casual question.

"Huh? Um, well, I mean—huh."

"Um, yes, well, that is—hmm?"

Their being so unsettled was something he didn't expect.

"...What were you doing alone together?" he asked in a suspiciously serious tone of voice.

"Alone together?!" Erika's tone was so disturbed it was funny.

"That isn't it!" Leo's tone could have been called a scream. "I was just in there practicing! She came later!"

"I came here to practice, but this annoying guy was hogging the damn thing!"

"Did you just call me annoying?!"

"Uhh, okay, I understand. I didn't mean anything by it."

The reality wasn't actually that interesting, but their reaction had been well worth it.

His mind switched gears. "Did you see any other invaders?" he asked seriously, though not suspiciously this time.

"I was protecting the teachers on the other side, but they're really good—they're mostly all taken care of," responded Erika, as though her previous fluster had never happened, in neither a serious nor light tone, but a calm one.

Leo was quick to change gears, too. "This may sound weird coming from me, but they're really third-rate magicians. Even three-on-one they couldn't put up any magic." He spoke as if it didn't matter, but taking on three people at once was no easy task in the first place.

This classmate of his seemed to be capable of more than he gave him credit for.

"Erika, is the office safe?" asked Miyuki.

Erika nodded. "They were quick to respond over there. By the time I arrived, the teachers had already tied up the invaders. There are a lot of valuables in there, after all."

Tatsuya found himself stuck on something she'd just said. He understood the office being a target of attack because of how many valuables were kept inside. But all that was in the practicum building were old CADs from previous generations. If there was any value to be found, it was the heat-resistant, vibration-resistant, shock-resistant building itself, which got away with just a few burns to its exterior after being hit with a grenade. If it had been destroyed, classes would have been obstructed for at least a month, but in the end, this was all that happened. If there were any other places where the school's administration would be hampered due to destructive activities, it would be where important equipment, materials, and documents were stored, since they couldn't resupply them immediately...

"...The lab building and the library!"

"Then was this a diversion? I did not expect such a broad scope. Could the resistance holding down the debate have been a diversion in itself?"

Tatsuya shook his head at the question Miyuki offered. "No, I think they were serious about it. I wonder if the coalition was just being used." He didn't use a word like *unfortunately* that would have shown pity toward them. That would be rude to those who were seriously clamoring for the elimination of discrimination.

"Anyway, the question is what we do now."

They had three choices: split up into two groups, go to the lab building, or go to the library.

"They're after the library."

Their decision was brought to them in the form of information.

"Ms. Ono?"

Low-heeled shoes, a slim-fitting pantsuit, and a lustrous sweater under a jacket. Her outfit today was completely different from the other day—it was meant for moving around in. The shine on her sweater probably came from metallic fibers with anti-bullet and anti-blade effects. Even her expression was drawn in severity. The air she gave off was like another person's.

"Their main force has already gotten into the library. Mibu is there, as well."

The three others looked at Tatsuya, confused. He stared right back at Haruka, though. Less than a second passed. "May I ask you for an explanation once this is over, ma'am?"

"I'd like to decline, but that won't be enough. May I ask you one thing in exchange?"

"What is it, ma'am?"

Haruka displayed vacillation, but she didn't get caught up on her words and waste time. "I'm asking you this as Haruka Ono, a counselor. I want you to give Mibu a chance. She's been worried since last year about the gap between her worth as a kendo athlete and as a Course 2 student. I talked to her several times...but I don't think I was enough. She ended up going along with them, so—"

"That's naive, ma'am." Her request was likely founded in an earnest awareness of her duties, but Tatsuya discarded it without mercy. "Let's go, Miyuki."

"Yes."

"Hey, Tatsuya!" Leo called after him.

And then, to a friend he couldn't discard, he gave one piece of advice. "If you have pity when you can't afford it, you're not the only one who gets hurt."

He didn't have time to say any more—and that was clear as he ran off.

Close skirmishes had unfolded in front of the library.

Aside from CADs, the attackers were also carrying knives and throwing weapons. There seemed to be a few students among them, but most were outsiders—invaders. The receiving end of the attack, composed mostly of seniors, had no CADs but had overwhelmingly superior magic power. The skill it took to go toe-to-toe with magic and without a CAD against weapon-wielding enemies marked them as fledgling magicians with hopeful futures. (And not so much fledglings as star rookies, they were.)

No sooner had Leo seen it than he dove in. Loosing a scream of "Panzeeeer!" he charged into the fray. There was meaning in his roar.

"Voice recognition? He gets more unique every day…"

"Tatsuya, was he just expanding and constructing a program at the same time?"

"Yeah, sequential expansion. It was all the rage a decade ago."

"Boy, even his magic is outdated…"

Fortunately, Erika's talking behind his back (?)—after having ignored the fact that the sealing magic she used was a technique of the past now—didn't make it to the fighting Leo. With his bulky, wide CAD that covered his forearm like a gauntlet, he stopped a cudgel being brought down at him and delivered a return punch.

I see. The CAD doubles as body armor, so I understand why it uses voice recognition—it doesn't need any moving parts or exposed sensors. Still, though…

"I'm surprised it hasn't broken on him yet," Erika remarked.

"He's using hardening magic on the CAD itself, too. Hardening magic works by confining the relative coordinates of particles to a tight area. However strong the impact is, as long as the relative coordinates between pieces don't go out of alignment, it can't be broken as long as its exterior remains intact."

"So he can use it as violently as he wants, huh? Fitting magic for a guy like that."

Erika and the others, trading comments for sneering, went around the melee toward the entrance. Leo, despite it, began a rampage, like he was trying to blow off steam. With his hands both covered by black gloves, he shattered the pellets and icicles flying toward him and went on smashing the shafts of metal and carbon resin. Sometimes sparks would fly. There were probably stun batons mixed in. There were thrusting knives he couldn't quite avoid, and some spring-loaded darts hidden in the enemies' sleeves firing at him to try and surprise him. None of them penetrated his white-and-green blazer.

"Is he hardening everything he's wearing? It's like he's covered in a full suit of plate armor."

The man himself had been unhesitating in declaring this his specialty. He'd clearly meant it.

By using a method of sequential expansion so he could both expand an activation program and construct and execute a magic program at the same time, Leo's hardening magic was being continuously updated.

The terrorists might have been armed, but they were still fresh, hairless amateurs in terms of how well trained they were. They wouldn't be able to pierce his armor. And his fists—they should have been punching with nothing but physical power, but the movement and acceleration spells he was using granted them exceptional destructive force. That kind of combat potential could be used right this instant in the military, as long as it was a close-combat skirmish where usage of firearms was restricted.

"Leo, we're going on ahead!"

"Got it! I'll hold 'em!"

Tatsuya left the area to Leo.

It was deathly silent inside the library. If Haruka was to be believed, then the attackers hadn't been repelled—the ones who went to intercept them had been blocked off. Nonfaculty police officers were normally stationed in the library, but it seemed like they'd been pacified already. Their competence was on another level, as might be expected from their "main force."

Tatsuya temporarily hid in a large closet beside the entrance, then expanded his awareness and searched for life signs. Not for indications of presence, but life signs.

Modern magic was a method of interfering with eidos, the information that accompanied events and the bodies that were one and the same with life. Everyone who used modern magic was conscious of individual eidos within the Idea—the information body belonging to the world itself, and the "information" platform containing all eidos had come to be called by a term from ancient Greek. But they were only conscious of eidos. There were few who could tell them apart. In exchange for normal magic talent, Tatsuya possessed a special, efficient perceptual ability that allowed him to distinguish individual eidos within the Idea.

"Four in the special viewing room on the second floor, two at the bottom of the staircase, and two more at the top…"

"Wow. With you around, there'd be no point in an ambush. I definitely wouldn't want to get on your bad side in a real battle."

"What could they be doing in the special viewing room?" asked Miyuki.

"For a hacking attempt, this is too docile. They're probably trying to steal classified information owned by the Magic University," speculated Tatsuya. "You can access private documents barred from the general public from the special viewing room."

Erika looked disappointed.

"Erika, you look like you've been let down," prodded Miyuki.

The girl took the opportunity to give her signature exaggerated shrug. "I'm not! It's just…a rebellion at school, youthful energies running rampant… I was kind of excited for it. But now that we know it's just some normal spy operation… I guess I just want my hopes and dreams back, you know what I mean?"

"Don't ask me. And you'd have been better off not having those dreams to begin with."

"But you just answered me!"

Tatsuya grunted, unable to argue with her. Miyuki hastily backed him up. "We must hurry to the special viewing room. Shall I perform an ambush?"

"No way, I'm gonna steal your thunder this time!" sang Erika before leaping out without waiting for a response like a burglar who'd just stolen a role in a play.

Without a sound or a hint, she urgently slid toward the stairs. Her baton, CAD embedded in its hilt, was already expanded.

The enemies had been waiting for an ambush opportunity, but instead they were assaulted. She brought down her baton, and as soon as they were struck, they toppled over backward.

Erika had taken down two enemies in an instant. It was a fully refined hand-to-hand combat technique, in stark contrast to Leo's wild fighting style.

At the sounds of their allies falling, the personnel lying in wait at the top of the stairs finally noticed she was there. One began to dash down the stairs, and behind him, the other began expanding an activation program. But in a flash of psions, the program shattered. The magician stood there, dazed, his magic having been negated. Tatsuya noticed the man stiffen up unnaturally, and a moment later he lost his balance and tumbled down the stairs.

"Oops…" grunted his little sister cutely.

"No problem," he responded curtly, returning his handgun-shaped CAD to his shoulder holster.

People who stand on two feet do so by unconsciously making minor adjustments to their center of gravity. If your body's movements were suddenly decelerated and forced to stop, you wouldn't be able to stay standing. They'd known that much, but Miyuki hadn't predicted the man would fall down the stairs.

Well, it doesn't look like he's broken his neck. He was part of all this violence, so he would have gone into this knowing he could get two or three ribs broken and maybe a concussion. That's what he meant by "no problem."

On the other hand, the second ambushing trooper came at Erika with not so much a *knife* as a real blade you wouldn't go wrong in calling a short sword.

He knew his face. He was the male student who had gone up against Sayaka as part of the kendo club's exhibition. Tatsuya could see a white wristband lined with blue and red on the right wrist he was using to try and break Erika's posture. It seemed as though the kendo club had been the first ones corrupted.

"Crap. Tatsuya...I need to...go easy...on students...right?"

Her question, spoken through a clash of locked swords, trembled slightly. The difference in physical strength born from their height disparity was affecting both of them, placing them in a stalemate.

"You don't need to *force* yourself to go easy on them," said Tatsuya, stepping toward them.

"No help needed here! No sir!" she said, stopping him. "I think this one's good enough for me to get serious."

She instantly upped the pressure she was applying, then let it go a moment later. Parrying her opponent had reversed their positions. She waved for them to keep on going. "Leave this to me!"

"All right."

The male student placed himself into a half-stance, on guard against a pincer attack. But the student didn't exist for Tatsuya or Miyuki anymore. Tatsuya launched himself off the floor with force. Miyuki launched herself off the floor with grace. Tatsuya's body bounced off the wall...and Miyuki's danced through the air. They landed on the upper floor at the same time.

Erika whistled in admiration as they left her and the dazed coalition student there and headed for the end of the hallway, where the special viewing room was.

Sayaka watched the work being done before her eyes with a complicated mind-set. Her allies, members of Blanche, were hacking into the only terminal in school that could access the secret documents—books and materials containing the very latest in magic research.

It was over half a year ago now that the boys' captain, Tsukasa, had mediated for her to be placed here. For some reason, Tsukasa didn't take her to Égalité, of which he was a member, but to Blanche instead. Sayaka hadn't intended to spread her own activities outside of school in the first place. She wasn't willing to even come *close* to getting involved with the law. Meeting them was part of her obligation toward Tsukasa, to whom she was indebted.

Tsukasa's older brother, who they said was the representative of Blanche's branch in Japan, had taught her a few things. Even now that she had started to think magic-based discrimination wasn't a problem that could be solved just by staying within school, her own focus of concern was the discrimination against Course 2 students.

She had actually wanted to participate in the debate. It wasn't enough for her to feel strongly about it; she wished to make her voice heard. Tsukasa had convinced her that this would be a more suitable position for her, though, so she couldn't decline.

What am I doing? she thought. They'd taken a key without permission, and taken part in hacking... Was this what she wanted? As she felt her thoughts beginning to move in a forbidden direction, she quickly returned her attention to the mission in front of her.

But they were supposed to be trying to abolish magic-based discrimination. Why did they need cutting-edge magic research materials for that? Tsukasa's older brother had told her that publicizing the research results of magic schools would be the first step toward abolishing discrimination.

But I don't really think letting people who can't use magic see magical theory would mean anything...

The question that had been pestering her came to mind again. Magic studies had no use for those who couldn't use magic. Magical theory was practical in a certain sense, too, so it didn't have any of the spiritual nature of religion. If there was anybody who wanted to reap the fruits of cutting-edge magic research, then wouldn't it be those who wanted to use magic…?

No, I'm sure there is research hidden in there that will benefit those who can't use magic, too…

It was a hypothesis created to satisfy herself. An answer she had been led to believe. But no matter how many times she repeated it to herself, she was never fully convinced.

"…Great, it's open."

There was a slight stir. Someone hastily produced a solid cube for recording data. Sayaka thought she saw a clear sign of greed cross her allies'—cross the men's faces, and turned her eyes away. Toward the door.

So she was the first one who noticed it. "The door!" she shrieked, causing the remaining members to whip around to look. They watched as the door was cut into a square, then fell into the room.

"Absurd!"

The surprised shout could have been called restrained, given the reality.

Stable, solid objects were not easily affected by eidos. The door was constructed from composite armor that could withstand a hit from an antitank rocket. Magic *could* destroy it—but to do that, whether by weighting, vibration, or dissolution, the magic program would need to be gigantic. It would require one of those processes to be layered upon itself many times. This instantaneous, quiet destruction should have been impossible.

As the men stood there frozen in both thought and action at the outrageous display, the memory cube at the one's fingertips shattered. Then, the portable terminal they were using to hack in with fell apart like its manufacturing process had just been swiftly reversed. The signal from the connected device suddenly broke off, and the viewing terminal locked itself.

"Corporate spies, I presume? Consider your schemes officially ruined," said a familiar voice, declaring the end in an indifferent tone.

Tatsuya held a shining, silvery, handgun-shaped specialized CAD. Gracefully sticking behind him was a slender person with her portable terminal at the ready.

Neither of the siblings' expressions bore any excitement whatsoever, and it almost made her forget they were in the middle of committing a crime.

"Shiba..." whispered Sayaka. She saw a right arm come up beside her.

Not in surrender—her ally was pointing a live gun at his underclassmen. The man was not a student of First High. He wasn't even a student at all. Their leader, Tsukasa's older brother, had directed them to bring this man with them. The carefully selected team member now looked hostile and ready to kill. Sayaka screamed silently. She controlled it so her voice didn't come out. Her hands didn't move. The realization that her ally was a killer scared her out of her wits.

But he didn't shoot. No bullet, capable of such easy death, came out. Instead, he crumpled to the floor, then writhed in such intense pain he couldn't even shout. His right hand still held the handgun. No, the handgun was *glued* to his hand; it was swelling up and turning purple.

"Please stop this foolish behavior. Do not think for a moment that I will overlook any malice directed toward my brother." The girl's tone was quiet, polite...and dignified.

She was so utterly *different*. Sayaka knew she couldn't stand up to her no matter what she did. Hers was a voice that froze any rebellious thoughts in their tracks just by speaking.

Next, Sayaka's paralyzed ears heard Tatsuya's cruel words. "Mibu, this is reality."

"Huh...?"

"An equal world, one where everyone is treated as good as everyone else. Such a thing is impossible. If there were a fair world where ability and aptitude were ignored, it would be a world in which everyone was treated equally coldly. You understand, though, don't you,

Mibu? Nobody can grant that kind of equality. It only exists as a sweet, convenient lie used for deceit."

Sayaka's unfocused eyes became focused then. Her underclassmen watched her directly, their eyes expressionless, but that slight hint of emotion deep inside them...

"Mibu, you've been used to steal the Magic University's private technology. This is the reality—the one you've been given by someone else, and the ideal that sounded so good."

Was it pity?

"Why?! Why did it turn out like this?" As soon as she felt that, some emotion she didn't really understand exploded out of her. "Was it wrong to try and get rid of discrimination? Was it wrong to want equality?! There's obviously discrimination out there, isn't there?! I'm not just imagining it. I didn't just imagine all the ridicule. The insulting stares. I heard the voices making fun of me! Was it wrong for me to try and get rid of that? Aren't you the same? You've always been compared to your perfect little sister next to you, haven't you? And you're being insulted unfairly! Everyone looks down on you, don't they?"

Her shouting was her heart's lamentation. It was a scream from deep in her heart. But it didn't make it to Tatsuya's heart. It didn't evoke sympathy. Everything she'd just said was the simple truth, and he accepted all of it without a second thought. The only things that registered in his mind were the definitions of her shouted words and the fact that she was shouting. He only saw that there was a girl here, wailing.

The light of pity Sayaka had seen was no more than something created by her own pity toward herself. She had hurled her words at the young man, but they hadn't reached his heart—instead, they came back to her own.

"I do not look down on my brother." It was a quiet voice. But in Miyuki's voice was an emotion to silence Sayaka's grief: anger. "Even if everyone else in the world slanders my brother, abuses him, and despises him, I will never change in my respect and affection for him."

"…You…" Sayaka was speechless. Miyuki's oath was so striking that it didn't only cut off her words, either, but her thoughts and feelings as well.

"My respect and affection have nothing to do with magic power. At the very least, the magic power the world seems to find so important is much stronger in me than it is in my brother. However, that fact holds no sway over my feelings for him. None of my feelings for him will be changed in the slightest because of something like that. Because I know that it's only one part of who he is."

"……"

"Everyone looks down on my brother? *That* is the unforgivable insult. There are certainly ignorant people who scorn my brother. But just as much as they scorn him—or maybe even more—there are people who understand how wonderful he is. Mibu, you are a pitiful person."

"What was that?" Her voice was loud—but without strength. It was devoid of feeling and emotion.

"Wasn't there anyone who acknowledged you? Has magic always been the only thing you've been measured by? No, I don't think that's true. I know at least one person who doesn't think that way. Do you know who I'm talking about?"

"……"

"My brother has acknowledged you. Both your skills with the sword and your appearance."

"…But those are just superficial things!"

"They are indeed just superficial things. But they are still a part of you. They're your charm. They're who you are, are they not?"

"……"

"Of course they're superficial. This is only the fourth time you've directly talked to my brother, after the two times in the cafeteria and the one time at the broadcast room. Only four times. What are you expecting from someone you just met?"

"Well, I…"

"In the end, the one most prejudiced against you is *you*. You are the one who looks down on yourself more than anybody as a failure and a Weed."

She couldn't argue. She couldn't even think about arguing. Miyuki's indication was such a shock that her mind went white.

And when people stop thinking...

...they abandon their own will.

After discarding the shed skin of one's own will, the whispers of the devil sneak in. No, in this case, the whispers of the puppeteer.

"Mibu, use your ring!" A man had been hiding, cowardly, behind a sixteen-year-old girl. That man gave a shout—almost a scream, in fact—and he swung his arm down toward the floor.

There was a soft *crack* and white smoke. At the same time, an inaudible yet stinging noise spread through the room. It was psionic noise. It was waves of Cast Jamming interfering with magic execution.

She heard three footsteps inside the smoke. Tatsuya stuck out his hand twice. Palm strikes, inside the smoke. His eyes were closed. There were two dull splats and two thuds on the floor.

"Miyuki, stop," came an instruction during the spare moment that came after.

The magic program Miyuki had been constructing immediately changed into something else. The wind whipped around, sucking in the white smoke. It was all compressed down to the size of a ping-pong ball, then imprisoned by dry ice that had appeared in midair, and fell to the floor.

Now that the room was visible again, she saw the three men lying prone. One man rolled around in intense pain from frostbite, and the other two had fainted, bruises on their faces.

"Tatsuya, was it all right not to arrest Mibu?" asked Miyuki, confused—but in no way guessing that he had an ulterior motive. Her suspicions of his relationships with women was no more than a silly, childish form of communication between siblings. She was well aware that Tatsuya wouldn't entertain that sort of personal feeling.

"I don't doubt your skills, but with as little visibility as we had, things could have turned out with an unexpected surprise. You don't need to take any risks—Erika will take care of Mibu for us."

If she chose the shortest route to the exit, she would have to bump into Erika, who was waiting back on the first floor. And from how the girl looked, she didn't seem to have enough mental capacity to take the long way around.

"I don't think there is any reason for Erika to get so zealous about it..."

"Not unless her opponent is Mibu."

Miyuki didn't really know why people got so hung up on specific enemies. To her, battle was something to be avoided first—and if that didn't work, won at all costs. It was the same no matter who she was fighting. Whoever they were, it didn't change the fact that they were an enemy. She only knew that there were people who were specific about who they fought, and that was all.

"I see. Erika will be fine, I expect."

So she left the girl to Erika, then decided to help her brother arrest the terrorist thieves.

Sayaka's actions were essentially reflexive. She'd been given the ring of antinite as a last resort in case she needed to escape. She was being educated in the usage of magic, so she knew the properties and limitations of Cast Jamming. In fact, she was more knowledgeable than most magicians at its application.

This ring didn't have the strength to defeat a magician. Cast Jamming could only disrupt magic—its only use was to avoid magic-based attacks. She couldn't beat that freshman with it.

She'd never seen such adept technique before. The freshman's martial prowess was now burned into her mind.

When she'd been given the ring, her leader had emphasized

many times that she should use the ring to escape. That vision was burned into her eyes, and the words carved into her ears, and they were controlling her limbs.

There were sounds of things hitting the floor behind her. There was nobody following her. She knew they meant her allies had been defeated. But with her thoughts paralyzed, she never realized she had the choice to go back and help them. She just followed what the manual said to do in case of failure—to return to the relay base belonging to a certain organization outside school. Dominated by that unreasonable but compulsive idea, she ran through the hallway and dashed down the stairs.

And there she stopped.

"Hello, there! Nice to meet you!"

A single female student—by the way she introduced herself, she was probably a freshman—was standing in her way, her hands joined behind her back, smiling in a friendly way.

"…Who are you?" she asked with clear caution in her voice.

But the freshman didn't change her cheerful expression. "I'm Erika Chiba from Class 1-E. I would just like to make sure that you are the runner-up in the national middle school girls' kendo tournament the year before last—Sayaka Mibu, correct?"

She found herself hit with a shock that she didn't understand. Somewhere in the shadows of her mind, somewhere in her heart where she couldn't see, she felt a pain, like she'd been struck with a *shinai*. "…Is there something wrong with that?" she asked in return, hiding the shock and her pain.

"No, not at all. Nothing wrong with it. I just wanted to make sure."

Erika was still standing with her hands folded behind her.

But there were no openings. Her body was slender, so it was far from blocking off the hallway, but Sayaka couldn't see an *opening* for her to slip by. And…those hands she hid behind her back—were they empty?

Was she holding anything?

"…I'm in a hurry. Could you let me through, please?" She couldn't feel anyone pursuing her from behind. But *he* probably snuck up on people perfectly silently every day before breakfast. Sayaka clamped down on her impatience and spoke to Erika as calmly as she could.

—Of course, she also knew there was zero probability she'd be able to just walk on by.

"Where could you be going?"

"It's got nothing to do with you."

"So…you don't intend to answer?"

"That's right."

"I suppose negotiations have failed," declared Erika, seeming to enjoy this. It was a silly way of making her point, but Sayaka was fully aware the girl was never going to let her through anyway.

Sayaka quickly looked to her left and right. Unfortunately, she didn't have a weapon. She had her CAD, but if she used magic, she would give up the only advantage she had—the Cast Jamming.

In her peripheral vision she saw a silver rod roll her way. It was one of the stun batons her allies had brought with them. Its reach was a little short, but it was a worthy substitute for what she was familiar with.

Slowly, imperceptibly, she dropped her weight.

She gathered her body's strength in her feet…and instantly leaped forward, rolling to pick up the baton. Then, without a moment's delay, she came up and pointed at the female student blocking her way.

Erika watched her, wondering what she was doing. "You don't need to hurry. I would have given you time to pick up a weapon…"

Sayaka's face flushed red. She cast a sharp glare at Erika to try and cover up her awkwardness and embarrassment at what was essentially a one-woman comedy act. "Move out of the way, or you're going to get hurt!"

"And now I have a proper reason to defend myself," she muttered, seeming to be no longer interested. "Not that I was going to use that as an excuse anyway."

She brought her hands out in front of her. In her right hand was an extending police baton, and in the other was a *wakizashi* with an actual blade. She tossed the weapon in her left hand aside.

"All right, then shall we begin?" she asked, bringing her right hand in front of her.

Sayaka assumed a stance again, with her weapon in front and her left hand supporting her right. She had a two-handed middle stance, while Erika stood in a one-handed half-stance.

It began suddenly, without any pre-match crossing of swords or shouts.

As soon as Erika saw her move, her baton flew toward Sayaka's neck. She immediately raised her own hands. With the defensive reflexes built into her body, she barely managed to stop the attack—and a moment later, her opponent had spun around behind her.

"A self-acceleration spell...?" she muttered. Erika didn't answer. "...The same as Watanabe?" Those words, however, caused Erika to stop. It was only momentary, but it was enough to turn things around.

When she went to take another step, an irritating noise on the floor stopped her foot. It was psionic noise, and she wasn't hearing it with her ears. Erika scowled, and Sayaka became the attacker.

She delivered a flurry of blows without leaving any time to breathe. Face, face, hands, torso, diagonal, upward, face, reverse diagonal... Her sword skills bore witness to the fact that she was not only well-versed in kendo as a sport, but in the old-fashioned ways, too.

She attacked like a flame. As fast as the wind, as quiet as the forest, as daring as fire, and immovable as the mountain, as the saying went. Her attacks were like a conflagration.

At some point, the psionic noise disappeared. She'd known that would happen. Cast Jamming worked by injecting psions into antinite. If you stopped the psion injection, it would stop emitting noise. The noise inside the room, too, eventually decayed and terminated. There was no way for Sayaka to maintain the Cast Jamming, since she was currently pouring everything into her sword attacks. It wasn't good enough to let her remain in a state to use magic, and it couldn't keep up with the speed of her sharp and fierce magic-weaved attacks.

And yet Erika still didn't try to use magic. Was she being pressured too much to build a magic program? Erika was a Course 2 student who struggled with compilation. Her CAD, however, was a specialized one with an emphasis on speed, and she was an expert at using this specific shape of CAD. And even under the effects of Cast Jamming, the supply of psions to her sealing spells was stable.

If she pushed herself off and got away, she should be able to activate the magic she specialized in. It didn't look like Sayaka was pressuring her enough that she couldn't get away. Her attacks were like a conflagration—but on the other hand, they were just as reckless and frantic.

Erika was handling them, blocking them, never moving more than she needed to. There was no impatience in her eyes. There was no disturbance in her breathing.

The first one to be disrupted was Sayaka, tiring from her attacks. The tables turned in the blink of an eye as the attacker and defender swapped places. One scraped past the other's finishing strike. As Sayaka stood there stiff as a pole, Erika flashed her own weapon across and knocked hers to the side. Her attack had been aimed at its base, and the stun baton, more fragile in construction than a wooden sword or a truncheon, bent.

"……" Sayaka stared down without fear at the police baton that was now in her face. A strong fighting spirit was in her eyes.

"Pick it up," demanded Erika without moving her weapon.

"……" Sayaka didn't understand what she was talking about, and couldn't answer.

"Pick up that *wakizashi* and show me everything you have. I'll crush the illusion of that woman chaining you down."

Despite the police baton in her face, Sayaka bent down. She picked up the *wakizashi* Erika had tossed aside before, then took up a stance again. But then, for some reason, she broke her stance and added her left hand to her right.

The brass ring on her right middle finger shone. She removed it and threw it to the floor. "I won't rely on that dumb thing. I'll defeat your technique with my own power."

Sayaka took off her blazer. Beneath the blazer of the First High girl's uniform was a sleeveless one-piece. Her arms were now exposed from the shoulder down—everything below her shoulders had gained freedom.

Then she turned the blade over. Striking someone with the dull edge ignored the construction of a katana, and she ran the risk of breaking it in vain. She took this stance despite the risk, showing her hesitation to kill and her discontent at having to dull her blade.

"I can tell," she said, taking such a stance and facing Erika. "Your skills—you're from the same school as Watanabe."

"My skills are a little bit different from that woman's."

They each exchanged short sentences, but from then on, silence ruled.

The silence gave way to tension, and tension to strain.

The very moment that strain crested, Erika vanished.

There was an instant crossing of blades. A high-pitched metallic sound rang out.

Erika's strike had been difficult even to observe, accelerated by magic as it was—but Sayaka stopped the blow. Stopped a single stroke.

And then the *wakizashi* fell from her hands. A moment later, she dropped to a knee, holding her right arm.

"I do apologize. I might have broken the bone."

"...It does feel cracked. It's fine. That means you couldn't hold back."

"Yeah. And you can be proud of that. You forced a daughter of the Chiba to fight seriously."

"Oh... So you're from the Chiba family?"

"Actually, yeah. And Mari Watanabe is one of our pupils. She's

in the register—but I'm a master, and I know the secrets. So in pure sword skills, I'm better than her."

Sayaka smiled a little at that. A fleeting, carefree smile. "I see... Hey, this is a little selfish of me, but would you mind calling a stretcher? I kind of feel...a...little dizzy..."

After those words came out, she collapsed to the floor. Erika carefully sat her body up and held her. As she lay there unconscious, she whispered, "It's all right. Your kind underclassman will accept the honor of carrying you."

"You want me to carry Mibu?"

Tatsuya asked the obvious question, but Erika nodded, not timid at all. "It's okay! She's not that heavy."

"That's not the problem..."

"You have a perfect reason for carrying a cute girl around. You should be happy!"

"That's not something I would get happy about... Wait, no, that's not the problem, either..."

"...You know, it's occurred to me before. Tatsuya, are you not interested in girls? You have *those* interests?"

"*Those* as in what?"

"Like, you're gay?"

"Of course not! Anyway, that's not the problem." Fighting a building sense of futility, he attempted a logical explanation that Erika would have to understand—though at this point, he could feel himself growing resigned. "We could just call for a stretcher. Why do I need to carry her?"

Miyuki just giggled.

"Because it would make Mibu happy, obviously."

Tatsuya found himself suddenly unsure of how to respond. With her being so unreasonable with him, persuading her with logic would be difficult, to say the least. In fact, he was at a loss for words.

"Why not, Tatsuya?" prodded Miyuki. "It may not be a race against time, but it cannot hurt to get her healed as soon as possible. I believe you carrying her there would be the fastest solution. Besides, you're making no progress here, are you? This is Erika we're talking about."

"Hey, Mizuki, what was *that* supposed to mean?"

"Sheesh, you're right. Guess I have no choice."

"Hey, Tatsuya, what's with the follow-up attack? Two-against-one is how cowards do things!"

"Oh, my, and here I was trying to take your side, Erika."

"No way! Lies, all of it!"

As though the pleasant (?) conversation between the noisy, loud Erika and the coolly reflecting Miyuki were his BGM, Tatsuya gently picked Sayaka up. He made sure not to jolt her around and disturb her.

"Huh. Yeah. You're really something, Tatsuya."

He didn't know what Erika was so impressed with, but she nodded to herself a few times. Getting involved with that would probably take a long time, so he just started walking.

Sayaka's face, in its unconsciousness, resembled a state of sound sleep.

After discovering via the monitoring function in his portable information terminal that the squad that had infiltrated the library had been captured, the captain of the boys' kendo team, Tsukasa, knew that the next step would be to contact the leader of Blanche in Japan, his older brother, and ask for further instructions. And as quickly as possible.

He was his older brother from another marriage, so they were stepbrothers, but right now he trusted him more than his actual parents.

He felt like he hadn't been happy at all with the second marriage, but at some point he'd come to and realized he was fine with it.

Directly after trying to consciously think about when that happened, his thoughts vanished into white noise. He realized he was spacing out for a moment (in internal time, at least), then shook his head, telling himself this wasn't the time or the place. It was too dangerous to use wireless communications on school grounds. They wouldn't be monitoring it or anything, so there shouldn't be anything about sending a normal message that needed to bother him, but this was an emergency situation. He'd be safer assuming all transmissions outside the school, whether through landlines or not, would be under observation.

Tsukasa hadn't thought leaving school would present an issue. Despite it being an emergency, it wasn't as though the country were at war, with itself or otherwise. There would be no gun fighting when he stepped out of school. They'd be strictly checking any outsiders before they entered, but they wouldn't obstruct a student from returning home.

Or so he'd determined—but unfortunately, he found his expectations betrayed.

"Is that Tsukasa from the kendo club? Goin' home already?"

As he was going to the main school gate openly, so as to not draw suspicion, a voice stopped him from behind. It wasn't a friend of his, but he did know the person. He turned around to see another senior standing there—one for whom the expression "scraggy" fit like a glove. The person wasn't tall, but he had a solid physique, all muscle and no fat.

On his arm was a disciplinary officer arm band. "Tatsumi... Well, with everything that's happening, clubs are canceled for today, right? I thought I'd get myself on home." Appearing agitated would be careless and foolish, Tsukasa told himself, managing to respond in a calm voice.

"Right. Well, that's true. It really isn't a good time for club activities, is it?"

"Yeah, you're right. I'll see you…" *later.* Tsukasa didn't get a chance to say the rest of it.

"Oh, one second. There's something I want to ask."

His heart leaped into his throat. "Me?" he replied, somehow hiding his surprise and making the best confused look that he could.

"Yeah, you, Tsukasa." Tatsumi's voice made Tsukasa more anxious. He felt like his tone implied that he knew *everything*. "Our chairwoman has this really *unenviable* skill, you see," he began, seemingly without any context—though it did nothing to lessen Tsukasa's caution. "She can use air currents to combine all sorts of fragrances. One of the things she can make is a truth serum, without even using anything illegal."

Tsukasa desperately bit back a shriek that was dangerously close to coming out. It was futile, though.

"You don't need to pretend everything's fine, Tsukasa. You know it as well as I do. Word's out—word that you're the one who guided them here."

Without another word, Tsukasa spun on his heel.

He might have been a Course 2 student lacking in magical ability, but perhaps as a result of his kendo training, he was confident with high-speed-movement magic. Though Tatsumi looked slow-witted, he was the best speed fighter among the seniors—but in a long-distance race, Tsukasa should have had an advantage.

So he thought, but his plan was ruined before he even took a second step.

"Tsukasa! I'm going to have to ask you to come with me, sir!"

An annoyingly assertive voice—or, more accurately, the voice's owner—stepped in front of him to block his way.

"Sawaki… Why are you two all the way out here?" His voice rose in a groan. All the commotion was happening in front of the library. Why would the disciplinary committee's big guns be here, of all places? It wasn't strange for Tsukasa to wonder about that.

"You didn't notice? We've been watching you all day. We got some help from a certain person who has remote viewing abilities. You didn't give yourself away at all, so we thought maybe we were wrong, but in the end, we saw you trying to run away."

As Tsukasa listened to Tatsumi talk happily behind him, he decided to force his way through. He'd have to go through Sawaki. With the situation he was in, going back on campus would be suicidal. But though Sawaki was only a sophomore, he was the school ace of magic martial arts, the term for magic-based close combat. Without a weapon, Tsukasa didn't stand a chance—at least, not in a fair fight.

Tsukasa pulled out the wristband around his right hand. Under it was a thin, narrow bracelet of brass—an antinite bracelet. He triggered its Cast Jamming. He knew that scattering jamming waves with the two of them there was the same as declaring he was *their* ally. But he couldn't afford to think past this situation right now. He needed to cut his way through this disaster and contact his brother. This was the somewhat obsessive, unreasonable thought that controlled his actions.

Sawaki grimaced as Tsukasa turned to him and charged. Magic martial arts were purely magical techniques to supplement one's physical body and grant powerful combat abilities. In a situation where he couldn't use magic, then even without a weapon, Tsukasa's skills as a kendo practitioner, which weren't based in magic at all, should have prevailed. That's what he believed as he attacked Sawaki with a bare-handed chop.

It was easily parried. There was a hard impact to his side—Sawaki's elbow was buried in his abdomen. He crumpled to the ground.

"You misunderstand, Tsukasa," said Tatsumi lowly and sympathetically as he looked down at him. "Sawaki's way above average even without magic. A lot of people make that mistake. But when you think about it, unless you can perform without magic, you won't be able to do much just by layering magic on top."

Tsukasa moaned in pain, unable to reply. Sawaki silently tied him up.

◇ ◇ ◇

In the nurse's office, Sayaka's questioning began.

Her right arm was still healing, and at first the school doctor tried to stop them from exciting her too much, but Sayaka had wanted to talk about everything now.

The student leaders of the school were all present at the questioning—Mayumi, Mari, and Katsuto. Kinoe Tsukasa, believed to be the mastermind, had been arrested, and the mayhem outside had, for the most part, calmed down, but they still didn't know any of the specifics. The outside invaders had been arrested and were being watched over by the faculty, who were going to give them over to the police. The student council president, club committee chairman, and disciplinary committee chairwoman, in their positions as students, couldn't get involved. On the other hand, Tsukasa wasn't yet in a state where he could be interrogated. Given the fact that their only source of information at the moment was being able to ask for details about the incident from Sayaka, it wasn't strange that the three of them had all gathered here.

Sayaka's story began from when she was drawn into her allies' circle.

About how last year, she had been spoken to by Tsukasa almost immediately after enrolling. About how the kendo club already had more than a few members who sympathized with Tsukasa at the time. About how it wasn't just the kendo club—they were holding thought education posing as an autonomous student magic practice circle. They had built up a foothold from inside First High over a longer span of time than the administration had imagined, and that fact surprised Mayumi and the others.

The one most shocked by Sayaka's story must have been Mari. She was shocked by something different from Mayumi and Katsuto, though.

"Sorry, I don't really have a clue…" Erika shot a thorny stare at the bewildered Mari, but she didn't have the mental leeway at the moment to notice it. "Is that true, Mibu?" she asked, confusion pouring from her voice.

Sayaka looked down, but not for more than a second. When she brought her face back up, she nodded, looking deflated. Then she replied in an equally deflated tone, "Now that I think about it, I was probably letting my title of *kendo belle* from middle school go to my head. So when I saw Watanabe's brilliant magic sword skills during an exhibition they put on to draw in new *kenjutsu* club members and asked you for instruction, it was a big shock how coldly you treated me... I figured you hadn't listened to me because I was a Course 2 student, and I got really down."

"Wait... Wait a second. The recruitment week last year, right? When I was roasting those rash people in the *kenjutsu* club? I remember that. I didn't forget about how you asked me to be your practice partner. I didn't treat you coldly or anything, though," she said, cocking her head in real confusion.

"People who say hurtful things don't usually know they're doing it, you know," objected Erika, her voice cynical.

Tatsuya stopped her, though. "Erika, be quiet for a moment."

"What? You're gonna take her side, is that it?"

"I said just be quiet for a moment. We can listen to comments and criticisms after her story is over."

Erika made a glum face at having had the door slammed in her face, but quieted down nonetheless.

After a brief silence, Sayaka, who seemed like she was struggling, argued, "You said I wouldn't even be a match for you, and that I should find someone who would be better for me... And to be told that by an upperclassman I looked up to right after entering high school, it was just..."

"Wait... No, wait. You misunderstood, Mibu."

"Huh?"

"If I recall correctly, this is what I said: 'I'm sorry, but with my skills, I can't possibly be a match for you. I would just be wasting your time. You should practice with someone who can match your skills.' ...Am I wrong?"

"Uh, well... Now...now that I think of it..."

"Besides, I would never tell you that you were no match for me. Your sword skills have always been better, ever since then."

Sayaka just stared at her with a vacant expression. Meanwhile, Mayumi asked Mari a question. "Wait a second, Mari. Then you declined to be Mibu's partner because she was stronger?"

"That's right. I might be better if we let magic into the argument, but...my sword skills are built around the principle of using them together with magic. They deal with how to move your body and use your weapon in a way that maximizes how effective your magic is. There's no reason I could match Mibu, trained purely in the way of the sword."

"Then...that was all...a misunderstanding on my part...?"

An uncomfortable silence crept into the nurse's office and slowly expanded.

"I must...I must seem like an idiot... I misunderstood you...and looked down on myself...and hated you for it... I let a whole year go to waste..."

Only Sayaka's sobbing could be heard.

Tatsuya was the one to break the silence. "I don't believe that it was a waste."

"...Shiba?"

He peered straight into her eyes as she brought her face up, then continued, his voice polite and understanding. "When Erika saw your skills, she said this: that the *kendo belle* she knew, who won second place in the middle school nationals, was so much stronger she was like a different person. Strength gained from hatred and bitterness may be a sad form of power, but they're your own skills that you acquired yourself, and no one else. You weren't obsessed with your bitterness, and you didn't lose yourself to lamentation. This year, you've greatly polished your skills of your own accord, so I believe it this year wasn't a waste at all."

"......"

"There are many different opportunities for people to become strong. You can't count the reasons for hard work in the hundreds or thousands. I think you only let the days of effort go to waste when you reject the effort, the time, and the results."

"Shiba..." Sayaka's eyes, looking up at Tatsuya, were flooded with tears. But behind them, she smiled. "Shiba, I have a request."

"What is it?"

"Could you come a little closer?"

"...Like this?"

"One more step."

"All right..."

The mood changed to one of relief.

But that...

"Okay, now please..."

...soon changed...

"...don't move from there."

...to one of surprise when Sayaka grasped Tatsuya's clothes tightly and buried her face in his chest and began to sob. Her sobbing quickly transformed as, clinging to his chest, she began to cry loudly.

As everyone present exchanged shaken glances, Tatsuya silently put her hands on her slender shoulders. Miyuki saw this and lowered her eyes.

After finally regaining her calm, Sayaka was able to speak regarding Blanche, the organization backing the coalition.

"It's just as you thought, Tatsuya," noted Miyuki.

"It was such a likely option that it's not interesting at all..."

"That's how reality is, Chairwoman. The problem now is..." The conversation was about to be derailed, but Tatsuya got it back on track with an especially uninteresting precept. "Where are they right now?" he said, as though their future course of action had already been decided.

"…Tatsuya, do you actually plan on having a battle with them?" asked Mayumi hesitantly.

"I don't believe that would be the right way to put it. I'm not going to have a battle with them—I'm going to crush them," said Tatsuya simply, nodding and adding to how extreme he was being.

Mari was the one to immediately protest. "It's too dangerous! This is way out of the league of a student!" She was always on the front lines when it came to dealing with problems, albeit school-related ones, but it was essentially a matter of course that she'd be sensitive to the danger.

"I'm against it as well. We should leave incidents not related to school to the police," said Mayumi, shaking her head, also with a strict expression. However…

"Then do you plan on sending Mibu to family court for attempted robbery?"

Their faces stiffened up at his words—they were at a loss.

"I see. Police intervention wouldn't be the best thing," said Katsuto. But we can't just leave them be. They might cause a similar incident in the future. But know this, Shiba." His glaring eyes pierced Tatsuya's own. "These are terrorists. Your life could be at risk should you be careless. Neither Saegusa, nor Watanabe, nor I can order a student of this school to put their life on the line."

"No, of course you can't," answered Tatsuya fluidly in the face of his stare. "I never planned on asking the disciplinary or club committees to help me in the first place."

"…You want to go alone?"

"I would, if at all possible."

"I will come," came the voice of his little sister without a moment's delay, causing a dry grin to come over his face.

"I'm coming, too!"

"And me."

Erika and Leo both expressed their own wishes to participate.

"Shiba, if you're doing this for me, then please, can't you stop this?" said Sayaka hastily, trying to stop them. "Why don't we leave it to the police like the president said? I'll be fine. I did something wrong, and I should be punished. If anything were to happen to any of you, I wouldn't be able to live with myself."

Tatsuya turned back with an expression unsuitable for answering the girl's sincerity. "I'm not doing this for you, Mibu," he said coldly and pointedly. Sayaka quieted, her face betraying her shock. "My living space has become a target for terrorism. I'm already a related party. I will eliminate everything that tries to harm Miyuki's and my daily lives. This is, for me, of the utmost importance."

He wasn't pretending to be the evil one so that Sayaka wouldn't have to feel any burden, either. Even those who didn't know him as well as Miyuki—Leo, Erika, Mayumi, and Mari—all grasped what he was really saying.

His gaze, like a glistening sword, *made* them understand.

It wasn't anger or a desire for battle—it was Tatsuya's confidence, or perhaps his determination, to speak of a future in which the terrorist threat had already been eliminated. Even Katsuto found himself unable to speak.

"But Tatsuya, how will we pinpoint Blanche's location?" asked Miyuki amid the silence. "I am sure they have vacated the temporary position Mibu knows of, and it doesn't seem that they have left any substantial clues." Only she spoke to her brother like she normally would.

"You're right. That goes for Tsukasa, too. Though it's not necessarily that they didn't leave clues—more like they never placed any to begin with."

"Then...?" prompted Miyuki, interested in why her brother didn't seem perplexed at all, despite saying they had nothing to go on.

"If we don't know something, we just need to ask someone who does."

"...Someone knows?"

"Anyone in mind, Tatsuya?"

Tatsuya shrugged off Erika's and Leo's questions and remained silent as the door to the room opened.

"Miss Ono?" said Mayumi.

In through the door came Haruka, giving a vaguely worried smile and wearing a pantsuit. "...I suppose I was naive to think I could completely conceal myself from Yakumo's treasured student..." she remarked openly, referring to Tatsuya, grinning drily.

He kept his face expressionless, but his voice in reply was subtly amazed. "You weren't trying to hide yourself at all. If you keep lying like that, ma'am, soon we won't even know how you really feel."

"I'll be more careful." Tatsuya invited her over and Haruka approached the bedside. She crouched down and locked eyes with Sayaka, who was sitting in bed. "It looks like you'll be all right."

"Miss Ono..."

"I'm sorry I couldn't help you." Sayaka shook her head at that. Haruka placed a hand on her shoulder, then stared intently into her eyes for a few moments before retreating from the bed.

"Wait. You know where these Blanche guys are, Haru?"

One might have expected the person who spoke to have said, "Who are you?" That didn't happen. Instead there came an unusual nickname Tatsuya had never heard that didn't fit the speaker at all.

"'Haru'?"

"Huh? Tatsuya, you didn't know?"

He probably thought it was a natural question, but upon being asked about it, Tatsuya faltered for a moment, unsure of how to reply.

"Everyone in class calls her that, ya know. Haru says she doesn't mind, either!"

"Not everyone! Only some of the boys in class call her that. Don't let him fool you, Tatsuya!"

"R-right..." The tension in the air lessened completely at this unexpected skit. But then he thought this might be better than people getting too tense for no good reason—of course, that was probably just so he could convince himself. "—Anyway, Miss Ono—"

"You can call me Haru, too."

"—Miss Ono, *ma'am*. Now that we're out of options, you can't feign ignorance anymore, can you?"

"You're no fun."

"……"

"…Ahem." Perhaps thinking her blank stare at Tatsuya unskillful now matter how one looked at it, she cleared her throat—this, too, was acted more than done seriously—and she adjusted her position. "Could you take out a map? That would be faster."

Tatsuya silently brought out his information terminal. He unfolded the screen and called up his map application. Haruka took her terminal out as well, one quite a bit more dainty and stylish than his own, and turned on its light communication function.

His map booted up and displayed a marker at the position it had been sent from hers.

"…That's basically right across town!"

"…Are they making fun of us?"

As implied from Leo's and Erika's indignant responses, it wouldn't even take an hour to walk there.

Tatsuya magnified the map and changed the information display. The marker indicated an abandoned bio-fuel factory built in a hilly area on the outskirts of town.

"…The factory was abandoned after it was discovered to be a front for environmental terrorists and they ran away overnight," he read aloud from the attached data.

"So they came crawling back while the authorities wouldn't realize it?"

"Meaning the groups are related?" Mari had phrased it as a question, but he could tell from her expression that she felt the same as Mayumi.

"If they left it as it was, then I suppose they didn't bring any deadly poisons with them," noted Katsuto.

"Yes. Our own investigations have not turned up any biochemical weapons," nodded Haruka.

"A car would be faster."

"Will we be detected with magic?"

"We'd be detected anyway. They're waiting for us to come to them, after all."

Tatsuya hadn't said he was a related party just because he was enrolled at the attacked First High. The terrorists had attempted to steal private magic technology. That meant they must have been after his own techniques, too. Kinoe Tsukasa attacking him was probably a test to gauge how effective they were. That was Tatsuya's reasoning.

"Straight in through the front door?"

"That would be the best way to catch them off-guard."

Tatsuya was one thing, but even Miyuki spoke belligerently, as though it came naturally to her, as they decided on their plan of attack.

Katsuto indicated his agreement with them. "Yes, that's an appropriate plan. I'll provide the car."

"Huh? Juumonji, are you going, too?" asked Mayumi—Tatsuya had been thinking the same thing.

Katsuto didn't look like the sort to stand on the front lines alone and not let subordinates participate. "As a member of the Juumonji, one of the Ten Master Clans, it is my natural duty. But above that, I cannot close my eyes to this situation as a student of First High. I can't leave everything to the underclassmen."

"…Then—"

"Saegusa, you're not going."

"Mayumi, the student council president needs to be here right now."

"…All right, fine," she said, nodding grudgingly to the two-pronged persuasion. "But you can't leave either, Mari. There might still be remnants in the school. What will we do if the disciplinary chairwoman isn't here?"

This time it was Mari's turn to nod grudgingly.

After watching the two female students' staring contest (?) Katsuto looked at Tatsuya. "Shiba, are you going now? It may turn into a night battle at this rate."

"It won't take that much time. I'll wrap things up before the sun sets."

"I see." Perhaps he felt something from Tatsuya's attitude then, because Katsuto didn't ask any more than that. He simply said, "I'll get the car," and left the nurse's office.

"I know the chairman and president are from the Ten Master Clans...but who is Haru, anyway?" asked Leo, though everyone else had intentionally avoided asking it.

Tatsuya shelved the question. "We'll talk about that later. Let's go!" Then he left the nurse's office behind, with Miyuki, then Leo and Erika in his wake.

The car was a large off-roader, and in its passenger seat was an additional member of their team.

"Yo, my man, Shiba!"

"Kirihara..."

"Man, you never get surprised."

"...No, I'm actually quite surprised." *At how you referred to me*, he thought, thinking better than saying it.

"Anyway, my man, I'm gettin' in on this, too."

"Go right ahead."

Tatsuya had no idea what was going through Kirihara's mind to make him suggest any of this, but there was no time to press him with questions. He just got into the off-roader, followed by his little sister and friends.

[11]

The world was painted in a madder red.

The big off-roader sprinted down the road, reflecting the evening sun from its body.

And then it smashed through the closed gates to the factory.

"Thanks a bunch, Leo!"

"…That… That was nothing."

"Ha-ha, you're wiped out!"

They had demanded high-level magic from Leo, such as suddenly hardening the entire big vehicle plowing down the bad road at over a hundred kilometers per hour at the exact moment of impact. He was considerably exhausted from the immense drain on his concentration.

"Shiba, this is your plan. You give the orders," said Katsuto, handing the reins and the responsibility to Tatsuya.

He nodded without a second's pause. "Leo, you stay here and secure our exit. Erika, you help Leo and take care of anyone trying to escape."

"Shouldn't we, like, capture them?"

"No need for more risks than necessary. Keep yourself safe and deal with them. Chairman, please take Kirihara and go around the left side of the building to the back entrance. Miyuki and I will walk in this way."

"All right."

"Sure, whatever. I'll slice up any rats who think they can get away."

"Tatsuya, be careful," said Leo.

"Don't do anything crazy, Miyuki!" urged Erika.

Both of them, ordered to stay behind, didn't complain about any unfairness.

Kirihara, brandishing his naked katana—though it had no edge—ran off, and Katsuto calmly went after him.

Tatsuya and Miyuki proceeded into the dimly lit factory casually, as though walking into a hypermarket.

Their encounter happened surprisingly early.

That was because Tatsuya had been advancing without a mind to securing cover, and the enemy had lined up on the floor of the hall-like room without concealing themselves.

"Welcome, and so nice to meet you," said one man, spreading his arms theatrically and bowing in welcome. "Tatsuya Shiba! And the lovely lady must be Miyuki Shiba, no?"

"Are you Blanche's leader?" asked Tatsuya indifferently. The man's age must have been around thirty—younger than he'd expected. With his gangly build and rimless decorative glasses, he gave the appearance of a scholar or lawyer.

"Oh, yes, how rude of me. As you say, I am the leader of Blanche's Japanese division, Hajime Tsukasa."

Tatsuya didn't feel any intimidation from him. The impression he entertained of the man, prejudiced though it may have been, was that of the common intellectual and fashionable revolutionary—big-headed and a failure.

But behind his exaggerated, narcissistic tone and gestures, there was a dark abyss peeking out. The thick madness Tatsuya glimpsed in it was something he'd expect the leader of a terrorist organization who fooled around with people's minds and lives to have.

"I see." Despite being aware of the man's insanity, though, Tatsuya's face remained stone cold. Hell and purgatory were no more than close friends of his. He didn't bother asking after his relationship with the kendo club captain, Kinoe Tsukasa. He just said two words and nodded.

He displayed his intent with his actions, not his words. He pulled the silver CAD from his shoulder holster.

"Hmm, a CAD. I figured you would at least bring a handgun with you. Very bold, very bold for you to come in here so openly. You may be a magician, but you will die if shot with a gun, you know."

"I am not a magician."

Blanche's leader opened his eyes wide with affectation at the unexpected response from the one he'd threatened to shoot. "Oh, I see. You are still a student! You seemed so very brazen I had nearly forgotten."

"You like to talk, do you? I suppose that's the selling point for an agitator."

"You're so young, and yet so strict. Is it not stiff, not uncomfortable to have such keen viewpoints from such a young age? At this rate, you'll suffocate on them before long." His tone and gestures were theatrical. His statement was self-absorbed.

But Tatsuya didn't feel like going along with Hajime Tsukasa's clown performance. "I will give you the option to surrender. Lay down your weapons and place your hands behind your head."

"Ha-ha-ha-ha-ha! Weren't you a Weed? Bad at magic? Oh, I do apologize—that is a discriminatory term. But what do you still draw confidence from? If you think magic is some sort of absolute power, you're making a big mistake." With a bout of loud laughter to make his lunacy even more pronounced, Hajime Tsukasa raised his right hand.

The members of Blanche lined up on either side of him, numbering over twenty, and all raised their firearms. Handguns weren't their only weapons—some even held submachine guns and assault rifles.

"Negotiations must be fair, so I will grant you the opportunity as well. Become our comrade, Tatsuya Shiba. My little brother told me about your Cast Jamming that doesn't require antinite, and I am extremely interested in it. This operation has us all working overtime. Just training ignorant students so we can use them takes quite a bit of time and money. It is truly and annoyingly difficult to forgive you for letting it all go to naught, but if you become our comrade, everything will be water under the bridge."

The thin smile on his face, the insanity disguised as sanity in his eyes—they would have struck fear into their target's heart were it not Tatsuya. If he hadn't been with Miyuki, she, too, would definitely have at least gotten goose bumps.

"So that's what you're after. You used Mibu to contact me and your brother to attack me, all to investigate that Cast Jamming imitation?"

"My, my, you are a smart child. How insightful. But you are still only a child—you understood all that and still came wandering in here. Having said that, children are stubborn creatures. They don't listen to what you tell them, even if they have zero chance of winning."

"What would you do in that case?"

"Let's see… How about this?"

He made a gesture that looked more like that of a street magician than a scholar.

Tatsuya's already-mostly-empty expression disappeared from his face as, seeming exhausted, he dropped the hand holding his CAD.

"Ha-ha-ha-ha-ha! You are already our comrade!"

Hajime Tsukasa stopped hiding his inner insanity, and he no longer evoked awe and respect—but he was equipped with a sort of charisma.

"Then for starters, why don't you put an end to your sister, with whom you walked here? She would want her beloved brother to be the one to do it!"

His commanding tone was not hastily prepared—he was quite familiar with using it.

In the past, he'd probably gotten many to obey him.

That twisted smile, that expression certain of his own authority.

"...Quit it with this monkey show. I'm too embarrassed to even watch."

But that expression froze the instant Tatsuya delivered his cold insult.

"Evil Eye, a type of outer magic that interferes with awareness. Or so it's nicknamed. It actually flashes patterns of light signals with hypnotic properties more quickly than humans can perceive them, giving them a direction and projecting them onto the person's retina—light-wave vibration magic. A simple hypnotic trick derived from brainwashing concepts, possible to create even with a video player. Because it can be performed without any grandiose machines, you can catch an opponent off-guard with it—but that's all it really is. If I recall correctly, it's a trick zealously researched in Belarus before the formation of the Federal Soviet Republics."

Tatsuya froze his enemy—not with magic, but with words.

"Was this what you used to substitute Mibu's memories, too?"

"Tatsuya, you mean...?" Miyuki's eyes were already wide, but she opened them wider in surprise.

He nodded, still expressionless. "Mibu's mistaken memory was so extreme it verged on unnatural. You do get shaken up after mishearing something like that, and sometimes people do fall into such an extreme misunderstanding. But normally, that cools down as time passes."

"...This... This trash." Wrath surged from Miyuki's noble lips.

Perhaps its heat thawed the man. "...You, how..." he groaned, appearing to struggle. He wasn't smiling madly. Now that the madness had withdrawn, all that was left was a slender, intellectual leader accustomed only to giving orders, never to getting his own hands dirty.

"You're a boring one." Tatsuya wasn't bothering to hide his contempt any longer. "Drawing my attention to your right hand as you took your glasses off, averting it from the CAD you used in your left hand... You think a parlor trick will work on me? I can tell what sort of magic you're casting by looking at the activation program, and I can deal with it. That shoddy magic you used? I only needed to delete part of the activation program. Without the parts describing the all-important hypnosis pattern, Evil Eye just becomes a series of lights."

He had no interest in exposed street magicians.

"Impossible... How...how can you... You bastard..."

"And you were speaking so politely before. It looks like your regal skin has peeled away."

It was then that Hajime Tsukasa finally figured it out.

This boy, when his expression went away—when he looked exhausted—it was because he had observed and nullified his spell and calculated he could consign Hajime to oblivion with certainty. The boy in front of him had never seen Hajime as another human, right from the beginning. He hadn't viewed him as human. His face, his name, his traits, his intentions—Hajime instinctively understood none of those had any meaning for the boy. They were nothing more than simple enemies to him. Obstacles. And now, by establishing his means of elimination, they weren't even obstacles anymore.

"F-fire, open fire!" He no longer had the leeway to keep up his appearance of dignity. His comrades—no, his subordinates—looked at him with misgivings, but he didn't have the leeway to notice them, either. He had been taken by a primordial, animallike fear as he ordered them to shoot the boy.

However...

"Wh-wha..."

"What is this? What happened?"

...not a single bullet fired.

Panic spread throughout the room. On the floor were the scattered, dismantled remains of handguns, submachine guns, and assault rifles. When the men had tried to pull the trigger, their weapons had reverted to their component parts.

And amid the panic, without attempting to quell it, Hajime Tsukasa ran away.

He completely ignored those at his back—his allies.

"Tatsuya, please chase him. I will handle this."

"All right." Tatsuya started walking toward the hallway farther in. The men naturally made way for him. Without doing anything, he arrived at the passage Hajime Tsukasa had run down. If they let him through like this, all that would need to happen was for the remaining Blanche members to be arrested.

But one of the members leaped for Tatsuya's back, a knife in his hand.

Or at least, he tried to. "Fool." Miyuki's sweet tones would normally prompt no end of fascination in others, but now they carried with them judgment without hope.

"Don't go too far. No need to dirty your hands with the likes of them."

"Yes, Tatsuya."

Between the siblings as they exchanged words, there was a carved statue covered head to toe in frost, which had tipped over and was falling to the floor.

Only one attempted to bring harm to her brother. The fool was already frozen solid.

For her, that alone was sufficient, and yet that alone was also insufficient.

The reason had been enough. The result had not.

The men before the single slender girl, numbering in the double digits, could no longer take a step. Their frozen legs could not move forward or retreat backward. Both mentally *and* physically.

The entire floor was shrouded with frost. Only within a small circle surrounding the girl was it the same season as it was outside.

The white rime swirled. The frost was creating cold. She brought up her right hand. Her form—the realization of an ice queen delivering judgment upon the deceased.

"You are unfortunate."

Her tone was different from normal. But her wording—her commanding, judging, authoritative expression—was not strange in the slightest.

"Had you not attempted to interfere with my brother, you would only have needed to suffer minor pain."

The cold slowly, steadily, crawled upward. Cold to dig into the cores of their bodies. Their faces blanched in dread and despair.

"I am not as benevolent as my brother."

The white frost had climbed to their necks.

"Now, pray—that you will at least keep your lives."

When the cold reached the crowns of their heads, it immediately increased in severity.

The vibration-deceleration wide-area magic, *Niflheim*.

Voiceless death agonies writhed within the frost.

Nobody was there to ambush him.

At least he was smart enough not to split his forces, thought Tatsuya. There was no point in sneak attacks against him—he could sense living presences. Hiding would have been meaningless, too.

There would be eleven terrorists still waiting for him in the next room. Eleven submachine guns. From the other side of the wall, he pulled the trigger on his CAD. Physical barriers were no obstruction to magic. With one of the only two spells he could use freely, Dismantle, he overwrote the eidos in the submachine guns. Once again his ears were greeted by voices rising in dismay.

He was able to sense living presences. He was able to analyze not only magic programs, but activation programs. But these were side effects of this spell and one other.

To perceive an object's construction, and to dismantle it.

For physical objects, he overwrote the construction's information into a state in which it was dismantled into its component parts. For a body of information, he just dismantled the information itself. It directly interfered with construction data; it was a spell counted among the most difficult magic in existence.

He had possessed these abilities since birth, though not of his own volition, so he couldn't use other magic properties. He could only create mock-ups. Virtual fakes. His magic calculation region was entirely occupied by these two spells of the highest level.

But right now, he didn't need a myriad of magic, just one absolute power that would bring him certain victory.

There were no weapons in his enemies' hands anymore. When he set foot into the deepest room in the building, he was not welcomed with bullets, but rather vacant laughter and unintelligible noise.

"How was that, Magician? This is real Cast Jamming!"

The lunatic darkness in his insane laughter that swallowed the minds of men was no longer present. Hajime Tsukasa's mad mirth was no more than the product of a bluff. Supporting his last-ditch effort was a bracelet of antinite, shining in brass on his right wrist. Rings of the same color adorned the fingers of the other eleven men as well.

Antinite was a military product whose production areas were extremely limited. Some examples included part of the ancient Aztec Empire, part of the Mayan nations, central Tibet, a portion of the Scottish highlands, and a part of the Iranian Plateau. Only locations that once held ancient mountain civilizations yielded it. It was as though it was a man-made object only refined at high elevations.

Tatsuya muttered to himself, looking at the massive quantities of it they had prepared. "Your patron is the re-secession faction in Ukraine-Belarus, and their sponsor is the G.A.A...." A shock passed through the room. *How utterly boring*, he thought. Third-rate was too good a term to use for them. He honestly couldn't stand being near them any longer.

"Do it! Magicians who can't use magic are just brats!"

Even fighting them would be a pain, so Tatsuya raised his right hand and pulled the trigger on his CAD.

It wasn't a gun. It didn't fire anything like it, such as lasers or charged particles, for which physical technology had yet to create miniaturized firing methods.

Despite that, the man in his line of fire collapsed, blood spurting from his thighs. From two spots—one in front, and one behind. The holes were small, like they'd been stabbed with thin needles. They struck their nerve ganglia directly, piercing their femurs.

Tatsuya pulled the trigger again and again. The men fell one after another, blood bursting from their shoulders, from their legs. He was drilling holes with a magic program that used his line of fire as a setting, dismantling every cellular substance making up their flesh—their skin, muscles, nerves, fluids, and bones—at the molecular level.

Changing just one part of an object or information... This, too, was a skill classified as being of high difficulty by modern magic, but for Tatsuya's magic calculation, which compensated for his extremely limited abilities, it was no trouble.

"Why?!" How many times had this man said that already? He would get an answer if he thought about it, but even counting would be ludicrous. "Why can you use magic with Cast Jamming?!"

Cast Jamming was a kind of typeless magic that created psionic noise to interfere with others executing magic. The composition of the noise created by the antinite hindered the usage of magic programs. Tatsuya had dismantled that composition and turned the noise into psionic ripples. Cast Jamming was an obstacle in the road to others' magic programs, and Tatsuya could dismantle the obstacle itself. That was really all it was.

Hajime Tsukasa was evidently a magician, given how he'd used Evil Eye, but he didn't even know this simple fact. At the moment, it was annoying to deal with this man, even to put an end to him.

Then, suddenly, the wall at Tatsuya's back split open. There was a subtle, glittering, silver light—the diffuse reflection of steel being vibrated at a high speed.

Vibration magic—it was the High-Frequency Blade.

"Eeeee!" Hajime Tsukasa jumped away from the wall, flailing like he'd thrown out his back.

Someone marched into where he'd just been standing, and it was Takeaki Kirihara. He must have come in through the back and literally carved out a path to get here.

"Yo. You the one who got these guys?" There was no other possible explanation. Before he could respond in the affirmative, Kirihara nodded a few times. "You really are somethin', my man. What about this guy?" he asked, pointing scornfully to the frightened man clinging to the wall.

"That's Blanche's leader, Hajime Tsukasa."

"So it's him...?"

The change was instant. Even Tatsuya winced at the wrath Kirihara unleashed from his body.

"So it's you! You're the one who cheated Mibu!"

"Eeeeeeee!"

"Mibu... It's all your fault!"

"Gyaaaaaaaaaaaaaaah!"

Kirihara's unsheathed katana sliced through Hajime Tsukasa's right arm, wearing the brass bracelet, at the elbow.

Katsuto showed up from the hole Kirihara had opened. He

scowled. Then, in the span of an instant, he used the CAD in his left hand. It was the same kind of multipurpose CAD in the shape of a portable terminal that Miyuki used. There was no time lag that could be detected with the five senses.

With the smell of burning flesh, the blood stopped, and so did the screams. Hajime Tsukasa foamed at the mouth, had a bout of incontinence, and fainted.

[12]

Katsuto took over cleaning up afterward.

What Tatsuya and the others had done had been excessive self-defense in a good light...and assault or attempted homicide in a bad one—not to mention their unlicensed use of magic. The hands of the law never reached them, though. The influence of the Ten Master Clans surpassed justice authorities.

When countries learned talent in modern magic was controlled by inborn qualities, they schemed to strengthen the bloodlines themselves. It was a logical consequence. For nations that only had enough power to research magic as a system, no matter where in the world they were, those schemes had been carried out since before the time modern magic and supernatural abilities were considered separate things.

Japan practiced it as well, of course. As a result, a new group was formed that would reign over the world of magic in this country.

That group was the Ten Master Clans.

They were not yet a century old, so their hierarchy was still fluid and unsettled. But that was a problem for the Ten Master Clans to deal with among themselves. A very tall fence had already been erected between the clans and everyone else.

There were the Hundred Families as well, who were seen as next on the ladder below the Ten Master Clans and strengthened their bloodlines in the same way. They, too, were across a gap so large they even admitted it themselves.

The Ten Master Clans would never stand on the political stage. They would not become outward-facing influences. In fact, they supported Japan on the front lines using their magic powers as soldiers, police officers, and administrative officials. In exchange for the abandonment of public influence, they had gained an essentially inviolable power behind the scenes of politics. That was the path this nation's modern magic users had chosen.

The most influential families among the Ten Master Clans were currently the Yotsuba and the Saegusa. Third in line were the Juumonji. If the heir to the Juumonji family was involved in an incident, normal police officers wouldn't be able to participate.

After the incident, Haruka was treated as though she were on a long-term business trip. As though—for it was a pretense diverging from the truth.

She had yet to answer the question Leo had asked her. Though considering the fact that First High didn't bring in a replacement counselor, she might have had plans on coming back at some point.

As part of the cleanup process, the door to the library's special viewing room—the one Tatsuya had severed using Dismantle—was being reported as having been destroyed by the Blanche operatives. That way, the school wouldn't have to follow up on a failure by key management. —Of course, the students hadn't reported to the school that Tatsuya had cut down a composite-armored door by himself, so they seemed to believe it at least half-seriously. The work being done by the school was to conceal the fact that keys had been stolen from the students. Even the fact that First High students had been part of it had been swept under the rug.

Sayaka's attempted spying, too, was treated as though it never happened due to adult circumstances.

* * *

Sayaka ended up in the hospital for a while. The fracture in the bone in her right arm wasn't enough of an injury to be hospitalized for. But when they found out Blanche's leader had been using Evil Eye, a light-wave vibration spell, the doctors wanted to keep her there for a while to make sure no effects from the mind control were still present.

Tatsuya only went to visit her once while she was hospitalized, but Erika visited frequently, and they became fast friends.

Kinoe Tsukasa, the captain of the boy's kendo team, wasn't charged with any crimes, either. He had been under the effects of some very severe mind control.

It was reported he was taking a temporary absence rather than withdrawing from school and was undergoing long-term treatment. He would probably end up leaving First High of his own volition, though. He had never really wanted to be a magician, and his pushion radiation sensitivity wasn't bad enough to hinder everyday life.

They'd discovered that Hajime Tsukasa had an eye on his ability to detect magic and made him enroll at a magic high school so that he could find magic that would prove useful to the organization. After his mind control wore off, he would likely strive toward what he really wanted to do—probably kendo.

Tatsuya's unique magic talents hadn't been divulged to anyone beyond the comrades who had gone with him to the abandoned factory. Mayumi and Mari hadn't been told, either. The same went for his friends Mizuki, Honoka, and Shizuku.

More accurately, Leo and Erika didn't know about the most crucial part of it.

Tatsuya didn't know what Katsuto had been thinking when he forbade Kirihara to speak of it, but he was grateful for the act all the same.

The magic he had—right now, it couldn't be public.

Of course, Mayumi and Mari appeared to vaguely suspect something was up.

Miyuki was depressed for a week afterward.

On the surface she was still the perfectly beautiful girl, but he'd seen her burying her face in her hands on sudden impulses.

—Only at home, though.

She must have been under the impression that using Niflheim had been going too far.

Fortunately, since the members of Blanche had coincidentally gone into a form of cold sleep—because of the properties of magic, even the freezing of internal parts of a body would happen in an instant, so no cell damage had been caused—it seemed none of them had been physically injured beyond the point of recovery.

When she was down, Tatsuya pampered her as much as she wanted, creating a situation that wasn't really funny but still had to be laughed at, where she seemed to take longer to come out of her depression instead.

At school, Tatsuya went about his business as usual. The disciplinary committee and student council had been making him do random errands, but he was finally well on the way to acquiring the quiet learning environment he'd envisioned upon enrolling.

And then May arrived.

On the day Sayaka was scheduled to be discharged, Tatsuya and Miyuki went together to celebrate at the hospital. (He decided to cancel his classes this morning. The freedom they had in attending lectures was a big merit of learning from a terminal without a teacher to supervise.)

When they got there...

"Isn't that Takeaki Kirihara?"

Tatsuya didn't need to be told—he noticed him, too.

Sayaka had already changed out of her hospital robes and into normal clothing. She was surrounded by family and nurses in the entrance hall.

Kirihara was next to her, taking part in the friendly conversation inside the ring of people. His face looked somehow abashed and just a little bit delighted.

"They are quite close, aren't they?" Miyuki noted.

She, of course, knew of the event that could have been called the beginning of everything—the incident in which the *kenjutsu* club had intervened in the kendo club's demonstration.

Seeing the main two concerned parties, Sayaka and Kirihara, acting so closely felt a little strange.

"I hear Kirihara's been coming every day."

"You don't say."

He turned around to the voice coming at him without any previous notice. Erika stood there, looking disappointed. "Gah. I guess you really can't be surprised."

"No, I certainly am. I had no idea Kirihara was such a sincere person."

"Not that!"

Tatsuya knew. He was obviously redirecting the conversation. So when Erika gave him that sullen look, he just smiled it away.

"Hmph! If you keep doing things in bad character like that, Saya's gonna dump you, y'know."

Tatsuya didn't pay much attention to the dumping bit.

He wasn't proud of it, but he had zero experience in being popular with girls.

More important—

"Erika... When you say Saya, do you mean Mibu?"

Miyuki was a step ahead of him in asking the question.

"Hmm? Yeah, that's right."

"...You seem pretty friendly with her already."

"Just leave it to me!"

Tatsuya almost blurted out *Leave what to you?* He decided that would just make this chaotic conversation even worse, so he stopped himself and swallowed his words. He'd come here for a hospital visit first and foremost.

Leading Miyuki and Erika behind him—though he wasn't quite sure whether Erika was following like she should have been, but that was a needless anxiety on his part no matter how he looked at it—he spoke into the ring of people. "Mibu?"

"Shiba! You came to see me?"

She made a slightly surprised face. As her expression bespoke of her not expecting this, the emotion melted into happiness and Sayaka welcomed him with a broad smile.

—Next to her, Kirihara looked sullen for a moment. It was an amusing gesture, one of the spices of life.

"Congratulations on being discharged." Miyuki handed the bouquet she held in both hands to her. At first Tatsuya had wanted to follow modern custom and have it delivered. Miyuki had been unusually firm in opposing the idea, though, insisting that there was meaning in bringing these kinds of things personally. He had backed down at her angry look and decided to yield.

Her holding a bouquet made her look so good that she stood out in the usual city streets because of it. But now that he'd seen Sayaka smile so happily upon receiving the flowers, Tatsuya knew it had been worth it to do as his sister had said.

"So you're the Shiba I've heard so much about, then?"

When Tatsuya had pulled away from the conversation between the girls—at this point he was just nodding along with them—a man of the age where he'd be in the prime of his life addressed him. He might have only been called by his last name, but there was no mistaking the look he was giving. His body was lean and toned, and his posture without deviation. Were they the results of martial arts training? His features, too, made him look like he was related to Sayaka.

"My name is Yuuzou Mibu—I'm Sayaka's father."

"Pleased to meet you. I'm Tatsuya Shiba."

"I'm his younger sister, Miyuki Shiba. Pleased to make your acquaintance."

Miyuki had been keen enough to notice Tatsuya exchanging introductions with someone, and bowed politely from behind him. Her elegant mannerisms seemed to make him falter a bit, but he stiffened his expression almost immediately, speaking to his training in martial arts.

Sayaka's sword skills were probably handed down from her father.

"Miyuki, could you look after Erika for me?" asked Tatsuya.

Miyuki turned around just as Kirihara was finding himself cornered by Erika talking to him. "Yes, Tatsuya. Please excuse me, *monsieur.*"

Her usage of *monsieur* gave Sayaka's father a start that he couldn't conceal, but he managed an acceptable response. Of course, both siblings pretended not to notice it.

Tatsuya turned back to face Sayaka's father. The man understood that his getting Miyuki out of the conversation was Tatsuya being considerate, so he didn't waste time with unnecessary prefaces.

"Shiba, I am grateful to you. My daughter is back on her feet because of you."

"I didn't do anything, sir. My sister and Chiba are the ones who got through to her. And Chiba and Kirihara are the ones who stayed with her while she was hospitalized. I did nothing but coldly refuse her. You may resent me for it, but I did nothing worthy of thanks."

"Refuse her? I couldn't even do that. I knew my daughter was anxious over her magic not improving as quickly as she liked, and yet I still didn't think it was an important problem. I was so caught up in my own measurement—that others' evaluation of one's magical abilities are completely different from strength in actual combat—that I didn't really understand just how much my daughter was worrying. In fact, I used how busy I was as an excuse. When she started associating with strange people, I didn't stand up and face it. I'm a failure of a father.

"I heard from her a general idea of what happened. She told me she began to doubt what she was doing after what you said to her, and it had been a long time since that happened. She said it was like awakening from a nightmare. And she was grateful to you. She said you saved her by telling her it wasn't for nothing. I don't know what she was referring to, but I do know that her gratitude was real.

"So just let me say this—*thank you*."

"...I really didn't do anything someone should thank me for, sir..."

Tatsuya shook his head slightly, a little uncomfortable. Sayaka's father shook his head. "...You're just like Kazama said, aren't you?"

That simple line was more than enough to take Tatsuya's calm away. "...You're familiar with Major Kazama?"

"I'm already retired from the service, but he's a friend of mine from life in the barracks. We're the same age, too. I'm still in touch with him."

Tatsuya understood from the man's previous words that he was pretty *closely* "in touch" with the major. He had to have been. Kazama would never speak of Tatsuya to a simple friend—even a close one.

"I consider it divine providence that Sayaka became friends with you. I honestly can't thank you enough for that. I would have liked a man like you to continue supporting Sayaka in the future..."

"...I'm not someone capable of supporting anyone like that."

"...We'll leave it at that, then. Forget it—that was just an absurd request from a foolish father. Of course, I haven't told anyone, not even my daughter, what I've heard from Kazama, so you needn't worry. I just wanted to tell you that you're someone capable of saving my daughter, and that you really did save her in the end. Really, thank you."

After he finished, he returned to where his wife was standing, without waiting for a reply—without letting Tatsuya abase himself any further.

He gave a slight shake of his head to drive away the not-so-slight sense of agitation he felt, then went back to his sister and the others.

"Oh, Shiba. What were you talking about with my dad?"

Sayaka addressed him immediately, as though he were a godsend, or like she was trying to find any possible way out of her current situation. It looked like Miyuki couldn't contain Erika by herself.

"Someone who took care of me long ago was a friend of your father's, and we were talking about him."

"Huh, really?"

"Yes, the world is a small place."

"I knew you and Saya were connected by fate!" Erika immediately involved herself in the conversation. She was on top of her game today, it seemed. "Hey, Saya, how come you switched from Tatsuya to Kirihara? Weren't you in love with Tatsuya?"

"W-wait, Eri?" Sayaka got flustered, but Tatsuya was thinking of something a little different.

Just "Eri," huh... He speculated that they had quite an affinity for each other—as though it had nothing to do with him.

"Erika, you're getting a little carried away today." Miyuki's rebuke went in one ear and out the other. This was beyond the point of being "on top of her game."

"If we're just talking about looks, then I think Tatsuya's got him beat."

"...You're a really rude woman, you know that?"

"Don't worry about it, Kirihara! It's not all about the face."

"...Seriously, you're gonna make me cry!"

"Whatever. So Saya, what was it? The sincerity? The kindness of awkward guys is pretty nice, huh?"

Sayaka's face went red all the way up to her ears. She tried to look away, but Erika would quickly move around her every time—probably using magic. Eventually she looked down, seeming like she was about to cry.

"Erika, maybe it's time—" *to give it a rest.* Tatsuya was interrupted in the middle of the act, though.

"Yeah...I think you're right," confessed Sayaka, beginning in a weak voice. Her inner turmoil must have reached its peak, her mental barriers crumbling. "I think I *was* in love with Shiba..."

"Whoa!" For some reason, the one most visibly surprised by this was Erika.

"He had this unwavering strength that I admired. But at the same time, I think I was afraid of it."

Miyuki glanced at him in concern. Tatsuya responded with a subtle, dry grin. Apparently his sister had taken to thinking his feelings could be easily hurt.

"It wouldn't matter how hard I ran, because I wouldn't be able to catch up to him. To become like him, I would have to keep on running forever. No matter how long I did, I would never get that strong... It may be a rude way to put it since Shiba helped me so much, but that's what I felt like."

"...I think I get it. Tatsuya definitely does make people feel like that sometimes."

"As for Kirihara, well... The first time I really talked to him was when he came to visit me here. But I thought I could walk along at the same pace as him, even if we fought sometimes. I guess that's why..."

"...Yeah, yeah. You make a lovely couple."

Tatsuya didn't know if he agreed with Erika's way of putting it, but on an emotional level they were of one mind. Back then, Sayaka hadn't just been pretending to be a cute girl—she really *was* one.

"What about you, Kirihara? When did you start to like Saya?"

"...Annoying brat. What does it matter, anyway? It's none of your business."

"That's right, Erika. It doesn't matter when it started." Tatsuya had been keeping quiet until that. But now, having said something a little mean-spirited, Erika turned around, a question mark popping into metaphorical existence over her head. "What's important is that Kirihara is seriously in love with Mibu."

"Wha—you—?!"

"Wow..."

"I can't say any more because it's a privacy thing, but when I saw Kirihara facing down Blanche's leader, I knew he was more manly than I am."

"I see..." muttered Erika. "Hey, Tatsuya?"

"What?"

"Tell me in secret later!"

"Chiba, you little...! Shiba, I swear, if you say *anything*, I'll deny it!"

"I won't tell."

"Oh, come on, what's it matter?"

"You stupid cow!"

Sayaka's parents, the nurses, and even Sayaka herself watched with loving smiles as the rampaging Kirihara chased the giggling Erika around the room.

As Tatsuya himself watched them actually start an all-out game of tag with slightly less-than-loving eyes, Miyuki quietly came up next to him. "Tatsuya?"

"Yeah?" he replied briefly, eyes still fixed on Erika and the others.

"Miyuki will stay with you forever—even if you run away at the speed of sound, and even if you pierce through the sky and soar up to the stars."

"...I'd think I'd be the one left behind, not you," he said, smiling a little pathetically. "But for now, we need to get our feet firmly on the ground before looking upward."

Miyuki gave him a mischievous smile back. "Are we going back to school?"

"Yeah. We'll have to stay late this weekend if we don't attend afternoon classes."

She knew he'd been speaking in jest. That's why she could smile, too.

But still, she couldn't help but ask something. She wanted to make sure. "Tatsuya... Isn't school difficult for you? With your real power, there is no need for you to attend high school in the first place... And you do it even though you're looked down on. If you're forcing yourself for my sake, I—"

"Miyuki," said Tatsuya, interrupting her question. "I'm not going to high school against my will. I know that I can only experience this kind of life now. I enjoy being a normal student with you."

"Tatsuya..."

"So let's get back to our normal life for today, shall we?"

Tatsuya, a little awkwardly, reached his hand out for Miyuki.

She happily took it.

—But in the end, Erika came crying to them when she didn't make it back in time for afternoon classes, and Tatsuya had to stay late that weekend anyway.

Chapter 1　Fin

Afterword

If you're able to read this afterword, then it means this book has safely made it out into the world. It still feels completely unreal to me that a novel I wrote is now a book.

In any case, for a lowly debut work, things got off to an *extremely* bold start with a duology right off the bat. And with only two months in between, too. At the time of writing this afterword, I haven't yet seen the actual finished article. I even had the audacity to suggest releasing both volumes at the same time, so I guess my desperate struggle on such a tight schedule was just what I get. I'd like, however, to start by apologizing to Ms. Ishida first and foremost, who got mixed up in all this (?), as well as the rest of the staff.

In all honesty, I was quite scared about whether some newbie with no notable achievements could really pull off the outrageous "continued in part two of two" business. I originally wrote this on media that didn't require me to be conscious of how many pages it was. I knew that if it became a physical book I'd have to either pare it down or split it up. When the editor told me I didn't have to pare it down, I was extremely grateful as a writer, but I was still anxious.

I felt again then that just the fact that it was irregular was enough to make me nervous. Of course, that nervousness did lead to me unhesitatingly agreeing with the editor when the two-month, two-book plan was brought up, so...

Speaking of irregularity, the main characters in this book, *The Irregular at Magic High School*, are all irregular boys and girls, some more so than others. My original concept for the main character, Tatsuya, was that of a youth labeled as a poor student because he couldn't be measured by a preexisting framework. The supporting characters are all irregular in some way or another as well. His little sister Miyuki, who could be said to be the other protagonist, is an honor student but certainly not normal by any stretch of the imagination... though I don't believe I need to elaborate on that point, since you've already read the book.

But while they all feel uneasy about being irregulars, it doesn't result in conflict. Both the main and supporting characters all defiantly think in a "so what?" kind of way. Actually, it might be less acting defiantly and more seriously not caring that much.

For heretics to push their heretical selves through and persist by force... There's probably some of my own aspiration in that as well. Heretics fighting through, without yielding to orthodoxy, finally running out of strength and being defeated and killed—the aesthetic of such destruction is appealing, but I think there's an important story to be told about heretics who calmly break all the walls in their way while saying "so what?"

Using a group of irregulars taken from both the honor students and the poor students—Tatsuya and Miyuki, Leo and Erika, Mayumi and Mari, and many others...

That was the sort of story I wanted to create.

Let's bring my talk of dreams to an end there.

I'd like to thank Ms. Ishida for giving beautiful illustrations to this work, Mr. Stone for patiently putting up with all my selfish requests, and all the staff involved in the creation of this book. Especially M. Ki—I sincerely apologize for all of my many shortcomings.

And my greatest thanks go out to all the readers who purchased this book.

I hope that you will give a look to the next book, *The Irregular at Magic High School, Vol. 3: Nine-School Battle Arc, Part I.*

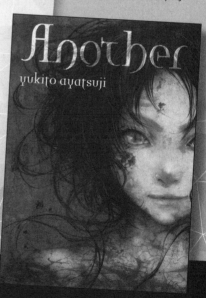